THE WEDDING GIFT

Regina Duke

PUBLISHED BY:
RD Books, Sparks, NV

The Wedding Gift
Copyright © 2017 Linda White

Publisher's Cataloging-in-Publication data

Names: Duke, Regina, author.
Title: The wedding gift / Regina Duke.
Series: Colorado Billionaires.
Description: Sparks, NV : RD Books, 2017.
Identifiers: ISBN 978-1-944752-10-1 (pbk.) | 978-1-944752-11-8 (ebook) | LCCN 2017944685
Subjects: LCSH Man-woman relationships--Fiction. | Family secrets--Fiction. | Colorado--Fiction. | Ranch -- Fiction. | Rich people--Fiction. | Romance--Fiction. | Love stories. | Romantic stories. | BISAC FICTION / Romance / Contemporary. | FICTION / Contemporary Women.
Classification: LCC PS3604.U43G54 2017 | DDC 813.6--dc23

Print ISBN: 978-1-944752-10-1
Ebook ISBN: 978-1-944752-11-8
Library of Congress Control Number: 2017944685

Edited by Marian Kelly
Formatting by StevieDeInk
Cover design by StevieDeInk
Cover photos from Fotolia.com

Chapter One

Outside Eagle's Toe, Colorado...

ON SATURDAY MORNING, KENZIE Shane pulled the classic cherry-red Mustang as close to the lip of the old marble quarry as she dared and turned off the engine. The setting October sun glinted off the new paint job. She ran her hands over the restored leather seats and squeezed the steering wheel. Her plan had kept her going, all the way from Denver. But now she was wavering. The car was all that was left. And she had paid for it, even though she didn't realize it was happening until the very end.

The sinking sun was forcing her hand. She pulled a screwdriver out of her bag, exited the car, removed the license plates, shoved them in her purse, and dropped it a few feet away. Removing the license plates had hardened her resolve. She opened the trunk and lifted her suitcase out. Her mind watched her body unload the car, as if her limbs were beyond her control. She fumbled for her cell phone and prepared to take a photo of the car in pristine condition. With phone in hand, she slipped back into the driver's seat long enough to start the engine and shift the car into neutral. It rocked a bit as she got out, and a frisson of fear raced along her spine. She didn't want to get dragged over the edge with the car.

Trembling slightly, she stepped away to breathe and give herself one last chance to examine her decision. All she could see was Todd's face, a film reel of his betrayals over the last year. She clenched her jaw and tucked her phone into the back pocket of her jeans. Then she moved to the back of the Mustang and began pushing it toward the edge of the quarry. Once she got it moving, it practically leapt to its own death. She fell to her hands and knees at the lip of the quarry and watched the magnificent classic car bounce down the cliff. At one point it struck an outcrop of rock and the back end flew over the front. It landed upside down at the bottom of the eighty-foot pit.

She listened carefully. Silence. The abrupt collision with the ground below had killed the engine, not to mention the other damage. Fists clenched, she shouted into the looming night.

"I'll never trust another man as long as I live!"

Live...live...live. The word echoed back at her from the other side of the quarry, as if urging her to get on with her life.

Kenzie stood as close to the edge as she dared, snapping another photo of the smashed Mustang. She toyed with the notion of finding her way to the bottom and getting better shots of the destruction, but the setting sun had already pushed shadows across the immense quarry. By the time she found a way down, it would be completely dark. She would have to settle for what she could photograph from the rim.

She replayed the events of the morning as the shadows swallowed what was left of the Mustang....

Todd woke her up at seven by banging on the door of her bedroom. Jerked out of sleep, she stumbled to open the door. "What do you want now? Haven't you done enough damage?"

"I'm just reminding you that you have to get out of the house by noon."

"Gee thanks, because hey, I guess I can't tell time on my own."

Todd smirked at her. "You're so dumb," he taunted. "You were dumb enough to let me take over your finances. So maybe you can't tell time either. But I want you out of here by noon."

"What's the big deal?" asked Kenzie. "It's not like you get to stay. Thanks to you, it's all gone. Thanks to you we've lost everything."

Todd actually had the nerve to laugh in her face. "Oh no," he said. "I haven't lost everything. It was your name on all the credit cards. We're being evicted, but I don't care. You're the one who wanted a house."

Kenzie looked around and grabbed the first thing she could find to throw at him. It was a hiking boot. It caught him square on the shoulder. It surprised him, but he recovered quickly. He laughed again, taunting her. "Is that all you've got?"

Kenzie stood there, fuming, and glared at him. How could she ever have thought this man was attractive? How could she ever have felt any love for him? She'd been so blinded by her attraction that she'd never even noticed his random acts of cruelty toward other people. She'd brushed off the fact that several times in her presence, he had dressed people down for no reason. She'd ignored the fact that riding in the car with him was always unpleasant because of the foul language he would hurl at other drivers. The turning point came when he showed her a semi-automatic gun that he claimed he'd purchased illegally on the street. She knew then that things were not going to end well.

During their year together, his drinking had increased, along with his spending. He always had cash and enjoyed flashing it under the noses of the bikers who came by for beer every weekend. But it was only recently that she discovered he was not spending his own money. He'd taken out credit cards in her name and ran up high balances on all of them. She didn't find out about it until the first collection agency began calling. Then came the second and the third. They kept calling and calling until she was at her wits' end. They never believed her when she said she didn't have a credit card because, of course, there were credit cards with her name on them being used almost every single day.

She stared daggers at Todd. "You have done everything in your power to ruin my life. I hope you reap exactly what you have sown."

"Oh, I'm so scared. Is that some kind of curse? You can't even come up with a decent string of swear words." Todd shook his head and clucked at her. "Too bad you're so darn good-looking," he said. "That's what kept me around. That and the fact that you're too stupid for your own good. How come you trusted me?" He sneered at her as if her naiveté was responsible for all his wrongdoing. "I was over you months ago, but hey, a man needs an income."

He spoke the words as if everything was her fault for being silly enough to actually trust the man she was foolish enough to fall in love with.

Todd had used cash advances from those fraudulent credit cards to restore his classic Mustang. He'd stalled her for months, assuring her he was paying the mortgage on their Denver house, when in reality, he was funneling that money as well into his beloved car. He kept it locked away in the tiny one-car garage out back.

Evidently, he forgot he'd given her a set of keys. When he first acquired it, the Mustang needed everything...new paint, tires, brakes, even a new engine block... in other words it was completely undrivable. He just wanted her to hang on to the spares. She'd tucked the keys in her purse, never expecting to use them.

"I've got some business to attend to," said Todd, hefting a hammer in one hand. "I'm coming back at noon to get my car. Don't be here." He punctuated his last sentence by poking a finger in her direction. Then he turned and headed downstairs. Every step was punctuated by a smash of the hammer as he punched holes in the walls.

Kenzie didn't move until she heard the door slam. She peeked out the window and watched him drop the hammer on the ground before opening the combination lock on the garage door. He went inside. A few moments, later he emerged, re-locked the door, got on his motorcycle, and roared down the driveway.

Two weeks earlier, her mother had called and asked her to come home and help out at the ranch. That was her window of escape. She hated the idea of moving home. But she no longer had a place to live. And there were still the debt collectors hounding her. She had no job, no money, no car, and no hope.

But she did have keys to the Mustang sitting in the garage. She slipped into her jeans and a clean tee shirt. Her suitcase was already packed. Socks and hiking boots, and she was ready to leave. The Mustang was Todd's prized possession. When he needed to drive around town, he used his motorcycle. He didn't want to get a ding or a scrape on that beautiful Mustang. The day her mother called, she'd dug in her purse to answer her cell phone, and her fingers had touched those keys. In that fraction of a second, she knew what she was going to do. She'd never done anything like it in her life, but then, a year ago, she'd been a totally different person. Todd had changed almost everything about her. When she met him, she was an optimistic young woman with a fresh college degree, ready to conquer the world. Now, when she looked inside herself, she couldn't find a shred of optimism. All she saw was pain and anger and the darkness brought on by his betrayal. She shouldered her purse and pulled her suitcase behind her, thump, thump, thump, down the stairs. She was numb. Not even the new holes in the the walls elicited any feeling. She pulled her suitcase out to the garage. She might as well have been sleepwalking. She picked up the hammer Todd had dropped and smashed the lock. She didn't feel a single pang of guilt as she opened the garage, put her suitcase in the trunk, and backed the Mustang down the driveway.

She drove to Eagle's Toe, where she saw the "Help Wanted" sign in the window of the Feed and Grain. After a brief interview—Taylor, the new owner, seemed nice, if a bit flaky—she returned to the Mustang and emptied the registration and insurance information from the glove box. It only took another half an hour to reach the quarry....

Now that the deed was done, all the fight went out of her. Weakened by emotional turmoil, she trudged toward her purse, stabbing out a number on the screen of her phone. She lifted it to her ear, waiting for her call to be answered.

"Hello?"

"Hi, Mom. I'm almost home. Could you come pick me up?"

"I thought you were driving down."

"I had a little car trouble. I'm on the highway, near the old Patterson Quarry turn-off."

"I'm on my way."

Kenzie ended the call and extended the handle of her wheeled suitcase. She looped the grip of her purse over it and pulled what was left of her life behind her toward the highway.

Meanwhile, somewhere in east Texas...

CLAYTON MASTERS STOOD OVER his father's ebony desk and pounded his index finger against its shiny surface. "You can't do this, Dad. It's not fair!"

Plano Masters leaned back in his oversized leather chair and stared at his son through half-lowered lids. It was Clayton's least favorite expression, and every time his father did it, he wanted to open those eyes. Maybe if he emptied that pitcher of iced tea in Dad's lap...that might do it. But he wasn't suicidal, and with his old man, the expression "My father will kill me" didn't sound too far outside the realm of possibility.

Plano drawled, "It's all in my name, Clayton. I can handle it any way I want."

"But you said yourself that Mother was out of her mind before... before..."

Plano steepled his long elegant fingers in front of his chin. "Before she committed suicide. I know it's hard to say out loud, but—"

"Obviously not for you," snapped Clayton, pushing his luck a bit. His sun-streaked blond hair swept back from his forehead with a grace and a wave his siblings all envied. His green eyes were the color of kiwis, his complexion was smooth and sported a natural hint of a tan year round. He looked like a male model, from his sensual mouth to his genetic gift of Masters muscle, the kind that other men had to work at for years.

"I will ignore that remark," rumbled his father, "given your current state of agitation."

Clayton paced to and fro in front of the desk, his fists clenched. "What about Austin?" he asked. "He got married summer before last. Doesn't that satisfy this arcane codicil? And if Mom wasn't in her right mind—"

Plano cut him off. "Enough of that. This was her wish from the day you were born. Long before her mental health deteriorated, she insisted that this be part of your legacy. As for your brother, Austin was the youngest of you three. This codicil applies to you, the eldest. And frankly, I think your mother was spiritually guided when she put this in place. For God's sake, Clayton, you're nearly thirty. Are you planning to spend your whole life partying on an allowance from me? It's as if your mother knew from day one that she'd have to insist on something like this."

"Spiritually guided?" Clayton snorted. "Don't you mean manipulated by our godmother?"

Plano slammed a palm down on his desk. "You leave Lulamae out of this!"

His outburst startled Clayton, and it took a few moments for him to reclaim his composure. He shifted his gaze away from his father and let some cockiness drain from his voice. "You've never fully explained her relationship to the family."

"Relationship?" He made a disgusted noise. "Lulamae was your Aunt Polly's friend, and she didn't introduce me to your mother. Polly did. And I knew from the first moment that she was destined to be mine." His eyes glistened with a distant memory.

Clayton finally dropped into an overstuffed chair. He never really thought his father would talk about Lulamae, but he'd needed something to defuse his anger. He knew that mentioning Lulamae would send Dad down memory lane. Lulamae was godmother to Clayton and his brothers, Austin and Dallas, and she played the same role in the lives of their cousins, Thor and Ulysses Garrison. Maybe he should ask Aunt Polly a few questions. It might shed some light on this ridiculous requirement for the transference of the family wealth.

Clayton wasn't sure what to make of his father's refusal to talk about Lulamae. The woman had power over their family and he suspected it somehow stemmed from his mother's suicide. Meanwhile he and his siblings had benefited from having a billionaire godmother. Birthdays were always delightful. She'd gone out of her way to make special visits to them when his father sent them off to boarding school for a while.

But in spite of all the wonderful things Lulamae represented, she also brought mystery and drama into their lives every time she showed up. Clayton wondered how much she had to do with this ridiculous requirement about the money he thought should have been his on his twenty-first birthday.

He snorted at his own question. It wasn't even a matter of whether she was involved, just how deeply. She was entangled in so many aspects of their lives. And yet, none of the cousins knew why. Clayton was sure he wasn't the only one to ponder these matters. Maybe he should go visit the Garrison side of the family. He had no interest in getting married, but neither had his cousin Thor before Ashley came into his life.

Thor's wedding had been fun. He chuckled to himself. Ulysses had drunk way too much, and so had Rudy. Those two were characters, that's for sure.

Although, since Uly met and married Belle, he'd settled down a lot. Rumor had it, they were getting ready to adopt a baby.

Hmmm. What was it about that little Colorado town? Two cousins and his brother Austin had gone there single and ended up married. Yes, he should definitely go. If nothing else, he could ask for advice about how to deal with his father's demands. Didn't Austin's marriage count for anything? He couldn't remember anyone ever pressuring Austin to get married. He just went and did it. On the other hand, Austin was still receiving the same piddling allowance that Clayton was getting. He had used his to set up his own photography studio in Eagle's Toe.

Maybe his father had been pressuring Austin after all, and Clayton just didn't hear about it. Either way, Austin ended up married. What was her name? Erin, that was it. She was a school teacher or something.

Clayton realized his father was ignoring him completely, engrossed in his investment portfolio. No point in hanging around. He'd already received the speech about how his allowance was big enough, yada, yada, yada. He said, "Bye, Dad." But Plano didn't seem to hear him. So he headed for the front drive where he slipped behind the wheel of his sleek, red Maserati Granturismo and let its elegance wrap him in the automotive equivalent of a lover's arms. If he started driving now, he could be in Colorado in ten hours. Sooner, if he ignored the speed limit and his luck held. His birthday loomed. The big three-oh. And if he didn't cave to his father's demands, he would live like a peasant on the dole until the old man died.

He cringed inwardly. Not a nice way to talk about his father. He really didn't want to lose his dad yet. His mother's suicide had changed his life forever. All their lives.

Memories of that awful week overwhelmed him as the Maserati's engine purred in his ear. And the face that dominated every memory, strangely enough, was Lulamae Franklin's. Surely his cousins would have some kind of information about her. They were all around the same age, although Thor and Ashley had two kids already. Was Lulamae involved in their children's lives as well? Most likely. He frowned at his hands on the wheel. Lulamae hadn't butted in when his cousin Axel's mother died a few years ago. Or had she? He had a flash of memory, a Christmas at Aunt Polly's ranch in Texas. All the cousins were there, having a ball with Polly's Doberman Pinschers, and lots of the Garrisons were there, including Uncle Rudy's brother, Lester, and his kids, Axel among them. Axel was actually his cousins' cousin, but when you're a kid, none of that matters. They were all cousins having a ball at Christmas. He remembered teasing them unmercifully for their New York accents, and they teased him back about sounding like a cast member from a western movie. At first, he took it hard. At one point, he ran into Polly's huge kitchen for comfort, hoping she'd make it all better with one of the iced cookies on the counter. But he stopped short and ducked behind the huge butcher block table when he heard his dad, his uncle, Lester, and Polly having words.

The subject of their argument was Lulamae. He was too young to understand everything he heard, but he could feel the raw emotion, and it was clear that Lester had no use for his beloved godmother. That had shocked Clayton so much, he'd sneaked back outside without even stealing a cookie.

He clenched his jaw. Time to find out. And the trip would placate his dad for a while. It would be an easy lie. "I'm going to Colorado to look for a bride. It seemed to work for Austin." That should keep his father quiet for a few weeks. On second thought, he would call his dad after he got to Colorado. It would give Clayton time to figure out a way to inherit his mother's fortune without ending his glorious bachelorhood. He was desperate and needed to figure out a way to get what was rightfully his. He needed that money. For one thing, creditors were hunting him down, trying to repossess his car. It wasn't even the most expensive Maserati, but the payments were too much for what was left of his monthly allowance after his other expenses.

One more little detail to tend to before he left. The engine purred as he steered the car around the tennis courts toward his father's eight-car garage. He knew the two-year-old Mercedes sedan was just sitting there, waiting to be traded in for a new car. He moved calmly, drawing no attention to himself. After all, he still had a room in the big house, and he used it at least one week a month. That meant all his father's hired help knew him well, and no would bat an eye if they saw him in the garage. He removed the protective tarp from the Mercedes. The keys were on their hook on the wall. He eased it out of the garage, then parked the Maserati in its spot and spread the tarp over the Italian masterpiece. No way would a repo team try breaking into his father's garage.

He smiled grimly as he programmed the Mercedes' GPS for the trip. They'd never find his car here, and as for anyone else looking for him, they'd never find him in Colorado.

Chapter Two

"MAMA, I ASKED YOU NOT to go to any trouble," grumbled Kenzie.

"Your room is the same as when you left for college. Keeping it clean was no trouble, not with you off at school." Marigold Shane stomped up the steps of the farmhouse.

"House needs painting," said Kenzie. "I can help with that."

"Your father will be more than happy to put you to work."

The grayness of her mother's hair shocked Kenzie. When she'd left for college, it had been brown, like her eyes. She followed her mother upstairs, her suitcase bumping behind her on every step, and noticed a slight gimp as Marigold climbed.

"I'll go take dinner out of the oven. You freshen up."

Kenzie hid a smile. Mom might be clutching the bannister these days, but she still sounded like the hardened country woman who used to frighten Kenzie's girl friends. She opened the door to her old bedroom and stepped back in time to her childhood. Her mother had seemed thrilled to see her, standing there by the highway with her single suitcase, and even sounded grateful that she had returned. Kenzie had a bad feeling about that. Partly because she had exaggerated a bit about her successes after college. She rolled her suitcase into the closet, then stood at the second-floor window, looking out on the farmyard and the barn. How did they do it? Farm animals had to be fed and tended to, nonstop, year-round. Her high school friends would look at her with envious eyes and ask how many horses she had.

None.

Her father was supporting a family, and there was never enough money to allow for a useless hay burner. She could raise sheep and pigs for 4-H and Future Farmers of America, but there was no way he was going to support her girlish desire for a horse.

She gazed down at the barnyard, dimly lit by a string of electric bulbs strung on poles here and there. Her father had spent the money to run electricity to the barn after one of her brothers stepped on a rusty nail while doing evening chores in the dark. They certainly couldn't afford another medical bill like that one. The lights were justified as a preventative measure. Of course, that meant that the kids had had no excuses whatsoever for not doing their chores.

Kenzie had spent her high school years dreaming of getting out of Eagle's Toe. She wanted to get off the farm, do something high tech, something in engineering maybe. She wanted an education that would allow her to live in Denver, and maybe someday even New York City. She wanted to get as far away from cow manure and pigpens as she could possibly get.

And here she was, back in her childhood bedroom, feeling like the biggest failure that ever lived.

Her mother's voice drifted up from the foot of the stairs. "Kenzie! Dinner is on the table. Don't let it get cold!"

She turned to drop her purse on the single bed she'd slept in practically her whole life and caught a glimpse of herself in the dresser mirror. She inhaled sharply, then let her breath out in a fragile laugh. For a second she thought she'd seen her twelve-year-old self looking back at her. Not a good omen.

But dinner smelled heavenly, and it didn't take much persuading to move her down the stairs to the kitchen.

"There you are." Her mother smiled, wiping her hands on her gingham apron. Was it the same one she'd worn throughout Kenzie's childhood? That couldn't be right. But knowing her dad and his attitude about money, she knew in her heart it was probably true.

"Where's Dad?"

Marigold averted her eyes. "He went to the Grange meeting. I asked him to skip it because I wanted us to have a little family dinner, like we used to do when all you kids were home, but he's so wound up about all this talk of oil and he didn't want to miss anything. You know John. If you smell dead fish, look out for the bear. He wants to keep an eye on those oil reps, and he wants to know if any of the other ranchers are signing leases." She carried a covered casserole dish to the table. "Four-cheese macaroni, your favorite."

Kenzie was touched. "Thanks, Mom." She sat down at her old place at the table. There it was again, that feeling of being twelve again. She shook it off as her mother poured iced tea into her glass. "I really appreciate you letting me come home for a while."

"Breakups are hard." Marigold said it like a woman with experience, but Kenzie wondered how she could possibly know. Hadn't she been married to her father forever?

Kenzie had been frankly surprised when her father agreed with her mother that their daughter should move home. He'd never faltered in his duty as a parent, but Kenzie'd always had the feeling that he couldn't wait for them to all get out of the house. Maybe he was worried they'd wind up living with their parents until they were thirty, like some of those families on TV.

"Did it take a lot of talking to get Dad to let me come?"

Marigold's eyes widened in surprise. "Oh no, dear. As soon as he heard you had sold your house, he couldn't wait for you to come home." She put a hand to her mouth. "That didn't sound quite right, did it? But it is true that we need your help on the farm. Your dad and I are getting older, and we just can't seem to get ahead. He had such hope in his eyes when I told him you wanted to move back." She dropped her eyes to her lap and said the blessing. "Lord, we thank you for this meal and for the blessing of having our Kenzie come home to help out. In Jesus' name, Amen."

"Amen," murmured Kenzie, feeling slightly awkward after being away five years. She would never tell her mother she hadn't said a blessing in that whole time.

Marigold lifted the lid off the casserole. A few chunks of sausage sizzled on top of the cheese and macaroni. The only other dishes on the table held home-grown snap beans and a sliced loaf of homemade bread. Marigold leaned across the table and said conspiratorially, "Save room. I made an apple pie!"

Kenzie felt tears burn behind her eyes. Was it Thomas Wolfe who said you can't go home again? In English Lit, she thought that was the dumbest thing she ever heard. Besides who would want to? But here at her mother's table, she was flooded with a bittersweet understanding of what he was talking about. She had gone off to college and then settled in Denver with Todd, her bad-boy ex. The last thing she expected was that she would ever go home again. And now that she was here, her throat tightened with feeling as the full import of those literary words settled around her like a hair shirt. Her mother was exactly the same as she used to be, only older. But Kenzie herself had changed more than she'd realized. And when she looked at her mother now, acting like it was a huge secret that she'd made a pie, Kenzie's heart ached. Six years ago, she couldn't wait to move away, and now she wanted to put her arms around her mother and tell her she loved her. But that would be so out of character, and her mother was never one for overt displays of affection. Instead, Kenzie helped herself clumsily to a scoop of macaroni.

"Don't forget your vegetables," Marigold crooned.

Kenzie smiled and took a serving of snap beans. "So Dad is all in a dither about those oil company offers? I thought you said on the phone that one of the Garrisons had offered to help you find a way to avoid giving in to the oil people."

"I'd say dither is a mild way to put it. He's just so worried about maybe losing the farm. And he was broken-hearted when none of you kids wanted to carry on."

Kenzie pushed her macaroni and cheese around on her plate. "Well, you may recall, Mom, that he never did much to make us feel a part of it all. We mostly felt like the hired help."

She realized a second too late that she'd said the wrong thing. Her mother dropped her gaze to her plate, and her voice regained the stern quality that gave all her pronouncements a steely finality.

"Your father did everything he could to make a successful life for his children."

"Sorry," said Kenzie meekly. She was in no position to start a fight with her mother. She needed a place to stay. At least for a while. "I know he always worked hard to provide for us all."

Her mother's tension dissipated and her voice softened. "I'm so glad you can finally see that, dear. Of course I shouldn't be surprised. You left here a scornful eighteen-year-old and here you come, all grown up and looking like you've learned some hurtful lessons along the way. You're such a mature young lady now. And when your father realized you were coming home to help us save the farm… and maybe loan us some of the money you made on the sale of your house… I swear he had tears of joy in his eyes."

Kenzie froze with her fork halfway to her mouth. Her appetite had vanished. The exaggerations she'd written in her letters home had grabbed her by the throat and threatened to choke the life right out of her.

♡

The trip took over ten hours because Clayton realized he needed to eat and sleep now and then.

15

His great-grandfather had made his fortune in railroads, but as soon as the winds of fortune changed direction, the next generation made sure to invest in a wide range of interests, not the least of which was land and oil in Texas. The Masters clan owned one major newspaper, three television networks, and—Clayton's favorite— two diamond mines in Africa. More recently, his father had begun investing in precious metals in Latin America. Clayton had visited a couple of the mine sites there, and he'd learned Spanish with the plan of living there, but the threat of kidnapping for ransom had made him very nervous. He didn't want to live like a prisoner in a cage, surrounded by armed guards everywhere he went. He'd finally talked his father into agreeing that the personal safety issues were not worth the risk. But he'd made sure he was highly useful to his dad by honing his language skills.

One of his brothers had studied Chinese, and Clayton was glad that one hadn't fallen to him. Not that he disliked the language, but the writing system felt overwhelming. Dallas loved it, though, and he was the family's main rep in China.

Clayton pulled into a diner in the northwest corner of Texas. Time to take a break. Did this mean he was getting old? Well, okay, older? His father was always saying it beat the alternative. But Clayton had barely begun to enjoy the finer things in life. And he loved turning all the female heads in every room he entered. Like now. The two waitresses saw him right away, and one of them let her mouth fall open at the sight of him. He'd heard his brother Austin refer to their cousin Thor as a Norse god once, and Clayton knew that description fit him as well.

Another reason to leave Latin America. He stood out like a sore thumb.

He picked a booth in the corner and slid into it, laying his phone on the table. He'd been watching the stock market app as he drove until he nearly ran head-on into a semi. Then he'd forced himself to shove his phone under his seat to keep from being tempted further. If he was so careless as to kill himself in a traffic accident, he would be one pissed off ghost. Or soul. Or whatever. After all, he had a rosy future ahead of him. Or he would have, as soon as he got control of his share of the family money.

He smiled up at the waitress pouring his coffee. She practically drooled. Of course, the sight of his car parked outside had made an impression as well. "Thank you, Doris. Just bring me a burger and fries, please."

"You got it, honey. Y'all from around here?"

Clayton answered vaguely, "Family's down near Dallas.'

"You're going the wrong way, sugar," she teased.

"I got a brother in Colorado," he said. "There's no escaping family."

Doris laughed. "Tell me about it. Cheese on that burger?"

"Sure." Clayton turned his attention to his phone. After a second or two Doris got the message and sashayed off toward the kitchen.

While he waited for his burger, Clayton decided he should give Austin a heads up about his pending arrival.

Austin Masters was not a Norse god. He'd been teased unmercifully in his teens for being a geek or a nerd or a dweeb. Whatever the word of the moment was. A counselor at their boarding school wanted him to be tested for autism, but his father put his foot down.

"I'm paying through the nose for you to educate my kids and take care of them for a while, not label them with something that could affect the rest of their lives."

Clayton figured the counselor was probably right, Austin should have been tested, but he was already thirteen. By thirteen, what difference would it make? Austin was completely functional, but he was painfully shy, didn't know a thing about combing his own hair, stuttered a bit when he talked, and earned every "geek" and "nerd" thrown his way, because he was a freaking genius. He fell in love with photography at school and never looked back. But what most people didn't realize was that he was also a computer whiz, and he manipulated Photoshop like Van Cliburn manipulated piano keys. Clayton was convinced that Austin's slight speech impediment was caused by a need to dumb down everything that came out of his mouth so regular mortals could understand him.

If Austin weren't married, Clayton would just show up on his doorstep. But he'd never met Erin. He was in Latin America when they got married. So he thought he'd better show some manners and not surprise a total stranger with an unannounced family visit.

Before his burger arrived, he texted Austin and asked if there was a decent hotel in Eagle's Toe. He also asked Austin to keep his visit quiet.

By the time he finished his burger, Austin had replied. "Looking forward to seeing you. Made you a res at the Cattleman's Inn under my name. Mum's the word."

He grinned at the screen. Bless his little heart, Austin was the best secret-keeper ever. That talent had saved Clayton's butt, literally, on several occasions when they were kids. In return, Clayton loved his little brother more than anyone else in the family.

His phone vibrated. Crap. His father was looking for him. He thumbed through the settings and turned off the location. No, he did not want to share his current location. Or his next one. Or the next one after that. He hoped and prayed his father had not yet discovered Clayton's automotive exchange. If he did, would he report the Mercedes as stolen? Clayton was sure his Aunt Polly would do exactly that, and they sprang from the same gene pool. But although Polly's impulsive behaviors were fodder for family gossip, he didn't really think his father would accuse him of stealing, especially since he'd left the Maserati as collateral. But it filled him with a sense of urgency. He had to get going.

"Doris, darlin', can I get a chocolate shake to go?" That would hold him for a while. He wondered idly if Austin could front him a car payment or two. He should never have taken his month's allowance to Vegas. What felt like a sure thing before he went had turned into a long night of losing at table after table. Not a great decision.

Not far from the restaurant, he spotted a run-down motel off the side of the highway. It was built long and low, surrounded by trees quickly losing their fall foliage. He parked the Mercedes behind the building and paid cash for his room, because credit cards were so easy to trace. In fact, he was carrying all the cash he possessed at the moment in a money belt around his waist. He could actually make one of the late car payments, but that was all he could do, and he needed travel money. And now, thanks to his father's stubborn streak, he needed something else as well.

He'd been giving his situation a lot of thought while he drove. Maybe it wouldn't be so bad to do what his father wanted. He mulled it over as he moved through the dinky motel room, turning on lights and flipping the TV to the weather channel. The place had a faint musty smell, but he was only going to be there a few hours. He needed to get some sleep before he finished the drive to Eagle's Toe. He satisfied himself that there were no dead bodies in the closet or the bathroom, then changed into sweats. He peeked through the curtain on the back window. His room was almost even with the Mercedes. Before, he'd been worried about the repo guys spotting his sports car. Now he worried that some doofus would bang into his father's Mercedes. That was almost scarier. He quietly swore an oath that he would never go to Vegas again.

He pulled the covers to the foot of the bed and stacked the pillows so he could stare at the weather channel until he drifted off to sleep. His mind returned to his inheritance problem. With a little effort he could find someone to marry before his birthday. That didn't mean they had to stay married forever. He shuddered at the thought. No, he could get married and then get divorced after he inherited. Ouch. He'd better get a good lawyer and figure out the safest way to do a prenuptial agreement. He didn't want to split his inheritance with some woman he hardly knew. He thought of Doris the waitress and shuddered atop the cold sheets. No, he'd have to find someone a lot classier than her. If he was going to pull a fast one on his old man, he had to think quality.

Chapter Three

BY THE TIME KENZIE'S FATHER returned from the Grange meeting, it was nine-fifteen and she had recovered enough appetite to have apple pie with her parents. Up until then, she had managed to keep her mother talking about relatives while they washed the dinner dishes together and she let her mother supervise her as she cleaned the stove. She frowned at the greasy mess and wondered what had happened to Marigold's spick-and-span attitude. She made sure to steer clear of anything to do with her life in Denver. Now she sat across the table from her father and had the definite impression that letting her come home was her mother's idea. His words said one thing but his tone told her something very different.

"Good to have you home." John Shane was a man of few words. As a child, Kenzie'd thought that made him rare and unique. The boys at school talked plenty. But after two years with her ex, hanging out with him and his friends, she realized that lots of men spoke very little. Some of them were reduced to grunts and gestures. Of course, she had to admit that those were the guys she liked the least, the ones who looked at her hungrily when her boyfriend wasn't watching. She was probably mentally assigning beastlike attributes to them because they made her nervous.

Her father was looking at her, waiting for an answer. She cleared her throat. "I can't tell you how much I appreciate this chance to be home for a while. I already told Mom I'd be happy to help you out around the farm. Maybe even help you paint the house?"

John cut off another bite of pie. "Good. That's the kind of help we can use. That and maybe some help buying the paint." He lifted a brow and glanced at her sideways.

Kenzie felt panic rising. There it was again. Her parents thought she'd made a ton of money selling that house. She hadn't been able to tell them the whole truth in her letters. How could she admit that she'd made a huge mistake? No matter how hard she'd tried, she just couldn't write the words—the stinking lousy truth, she thought—and so she led them along with vague invented details about the realtor and showings and offers being made and withdrawn.

She hadn't started out to deceive them. She never thought she'd end up coming home. The chances of them ever learning the truth had seemed so miniscule. But now here she was, sitting in her mother's kitchen, trying to maintain eye contact with her father while talking about the passel of lies she'd filled her letters with. At some point, she'd have to tell them everything, but not tonight. She knew that if she laid the whole mess out right this moment, they'd be up all night talking and shouting and making threats against the man who had done her wrong—or even worse, telling her how stupid she'd been to trust him—and she just couldn't face that yet. She wanted to crawl into bed and hide under the blankets—*I hope they still smell like sunshine and fresh air*—and think about nothing for a while.

"I'm pretty tired," she said, smashing pie shell crumbs with her fork. "I should go to bed soon. Before my car died on me,..." She almost choked on the lie and had to clear her throat. "...I stopped in Eagle's Toe and applied for a job. I start Monday. So I should be able to buy the paint for the house." She looked hopefully at her mother.

But John made a noise. "How do you plan to help with chores if you go to work in town every day?"

Kenzie swallowed her irritation. Same old Dad. Nothing was good enough. She licked her fork clean before responding. "Actually, I start at ten. I asked for a late start so I can get up early and help you and Mom before I go." She bit her bottom lip. "Since my car died"—a deserving death—"I was hoping you'd let me drive the old truck until I can get another vehicle."

John washed his bite of pie down with a swig of milk. Kenzie held her breath, wondering how he would react to her request. Much to her relief, he nodded.

"That sounds fair. What time will you be getting off?"

"Four. So I can be here for evening chores, too."

The tension in the air seemed to evaporate. She'd guessed right. They really needed an extra pair of hands, and they obviously couldn't afford to pay for hired help.

Marigold added, "And I'm sure she plans to contribute to the groceries and such." She nodded encouragingly.

Kenzie agreed. "Of course."

John said, "Good. Have you been talking your mother's ears off about your breakup?"

"She's hardly even spoken of it," said Marigold. She added pointedly, "And we won't ask for details until she's ready to share."

Kenzie dropped her gaze to hide her smile. Did Dad even know how many decisions Mom made for him? In this case, she was very grateful. She covered a yawn with one hand. "If it's all right, I'll say goodnight. What time do you get started in the morning, Dad?"

"I will knock on your door at five. Animals can't wait."

That's my father, she thought. She planted a dry kiss on her mother's cheek and started to do the same to John, but he raised a callused hand and brushed her away.

"No need to kiss up. I'm grateful to have you back. Lots to do. Good to have a full day tomorrow before you start your job."

"Okay then. Goodnight." She headed upstairs. Before she reached the first landing, she could hear them talking in hushed tones. She couldn't make out much more than her name, but it was clear that her mother was still convincing her father that having her around would be a good thing. At least she hoped she was. Her mother's voice was sweet and cajoling, a tone she never used with her children. Her father's tone was curt, and he sounded really tired. When their conversation paused, she rushed to her room so they wouldn't find out she'd been standing there, trying to eavesdrop.

She changed into her favorite pajamas—red flannels with galloping horses on them—and crawled into bed. She didn't bother to check her phone. She didn't want to hear any more begging, threatening, or ranting. She lay there, staring at the same ceiling she'd stared at every night while growing up, and wondered what her parents would do when they found out what had really happened in Denver. It was best not to think too much about it. She'd just have to make sure she was so helpful to them that they could find it in their hearts to forgive her.

♡

Kenzie figured after five o'clock chores on Sunday morning, the day would be filled with work. She was surprised and mildly alarmed when, after the animals were cared for, Dad settled in his recliner and used the remote to find a sports channel. He settled on MLB, and within minutes, he had dozed off.

Marigold seemed to think that was normal behavior, so Kenzie didn't pry. But neither did she enjoy the slow pace of the household. "Are you making bread today, Mom?"

"Yes, I thought I'd get a couple of loaves ready for the oven."

Kenzie smiled. "Homemade bread is something I've missed terribly."

"You can help me get it ready. I'll just have one more cup of coffee."

Kenzie began to fidget. "Okay, Mom. I'll run upstairs and vacuum. Will the noise bother Dad?"

"Oh, no. He can sleep through anything lately."

Kenzie vacuumed the entire upper floor. She was surprised by the amount of dust on the surfaces. When she was in high school, her mother used to check her room before she could go anywhere with her friends on Saturdays. But they were getting older. And that tended to slow people down.

She went downstairs and found her mother still sipping at her coffee. A local paper was spread out on the table in front of her. The breakfast dishes were stacked in the sink.

"I'll take care of these dishes for you, Mom."

"Thank you, dear."

"Anything important in the paper?"

"It looks like Kevin Fineman Wake is thinking about running for a state office. The ladies at the Grange told me his mother, Krystal, wants him to run for governor." She made an "oo-la-la" face.

"Didn't you and Dad go to school with Krystal Fineman?" She ran warm water into the sink.

"Yep. Things are different these days. But there's a private academy in town now, and even though it's open to everyone, the tuition means only the wealthier families can send their kids. Krystal's parents sent her to our regular high school. But she's still really sweet with us. Whenever your dad needed to sell off cattle, Krystal was right there, giving him top dollar."

Kenzie added more dish soap and began stacking the clean dishes in the rack. "I was surprised to see so few cattle in the field. And what happened to Old Toro?"

"Poor old bull caught pneumonia. We thought he'd pull through, but he was getting on in years and your father found him dead one morning." Marigold shook her head. "That was such a blow to your dad.

He keeps saying he'll do that artificial insemination, but last year, only three calves were born."

"And the goats?" Kenzie rinsed the last dish.

"What about them?"

"Well, there are only a few left. And no sheep at all. I thought you were selling wool and goat's milk?"

Marigold turned a page and answered without looking up from the paper. "Shearing sheep is hard work. And the dogs were getting so old, they couldn't really do their jobs anymore. They're just pets now. Couch potatoes."

Kenzie sat down at the table, wiping her hands on a dish towel. "Gee, I feel so out of touch. When I came home for holidays, you never talked much about this stuff."

Marigold pinned her with a motherly stare. "You were so busy talking about your boyfriend and your classmates, it never seemed the right time to bring up the livestock. Besides, you'd only stay two days at Christmas. Hardly enough time for hello and goodbye."

Kenzie felt a strange sense of relief that her mother could still make her feel guilty with a word and a tone of voice. "Sorry. I guess I haven't been the most considerate daughter."

"Don't worry," said Marigold softly. "Your sister and your brothers haven't exactly been beating down the door."

"Yeah, but they're all in the service." She pulled a piece off a cinnamon roll and contemplated eating it. "When I left home, I was ready to get away. And now, looking back, I feel like I was such a brat and so unappreciative."

"Your father and I were young once. We understand. We're just delighted to have you back now." She tilted her head, as if thrown off balance by the question she wanted to ask. "Will you make a lot of money from selling your house in Denver?"

Kenzie's insides tightened into a knot. She cleared her throat. "I'm not sure how it will all play out, Mom. But as soon as I hear any news, I'll let you know. Don't worry. Anything I get, I will share with you and Dad." She added silently, *What a lousy promise when you know you have nothing coming.* She needed to change the subject. "I heard the washer going earlier. Can I hang out clothes for you?"

"That would be lovely."

Kenzie smiled and headed for the laundry room, grateful not to have to answer any more questions. She spent most of Sunday doing chores inside and out, feeling sad that her mother—once a scrupulous housekeeper—was now settling for "clean enough." She wondered if the measly income from her new job would really be much of a help.

♡

Clayton was pleased with the room reserved for him at the Cattleman's, and he was grateful that the person at the registration desk had let him sign in before three o'clock. He hadn't slept well at that cheap hotel, and the light Sunday traffic was a blessing. He knew that Austin would pick something middle-of-the-road, but with quality in mind. That was good, because Clayton wasn't sure that his credit card would cover the cost of a luxury suite. Another result of his craziness in Vegas.

"Note to self," he said wryly. "Drinking and dice do not make a good combination." He tried not to think about how much money he'd left on the craps table and forced himself to appreciate the upscale decor of his accommodations.

It was certainly a step up from the motel room he'd spend the night in. In fact the difference was night and day. He shuddered at the memory of that shabby little room and wondered if that was what was in store for him for the rest of his life? He definitely had to figure out a way to get his hands on his share of his inheritance. And if that meant arranging to marry someone just to please his father and conform to a ludicrous requirement, then that was what he would have to do. He was tired of looking over his shoulder, wondering when the repossession team was going to catch up with him and take the Maserati. If they did, he would be faced with trying to find some kind of transportation that was more in keeping with his current financial status. And that was unacceptable.

"A man has his pride," he declared to the parking lot below. Then he snorted. "But not much of it anymore," he mumbled, scanning the lot for his car. There it was. Still safe and sound.

His room was halfway up the tower on the west end of the hotel. He had seen a coffee shop and a nice restaurant on the ground floor where he could have dinner. But he wasn't ready to leave the hotel room yet. He just wandered around, looking at all the amenities and reminding himself that he was not a peon. And as he did so, he grew angrier at his father for insisting that he would not come into his inheritance until he was safely married and settled down. What old-fashioned nonsense!

Well, Clayton had news for his father. He would get married, and as soon as he had full control of his finances, he would arrange for a quick and easy divorce. He jotted a reminder to himself to hire a lawyer. Then he remembered that if he contacted one of the family retainers, his father would hear all about it. No, that wouldn't do. He would have to find a local lawyer, someone his father didn't know about, in order to arrange the appropriate legal documents that would save his imminent fortune from ending up in the hands of the woman he eventually married and divorced.

He finally had dinner in the Cattleman's Italian restaurant, Il Vaccaro. The chicken parmesan was excellent and the bread was to die for. He ate way more than he should have, and was going to skip dessert, but the waiter explained that the chocolate cheesecake was famous all over Colorado, and he really should try it. So he lingered over dessert and coffee.

Clayton ignored the uneasy feeling that what he was contemplating was in opposition to everything he'd grown up believing in. Ordinarily, he was not a tricky person. Deceit was new to him. None of this came easily. But he really needed a source of income that would match his status. He didn't mind working for a living, but no one wanted to pay him what he thought he was worth. That made finding a job pretty difficult. His father wanted him to work in one of the family businesses, wedged tightly under Daddy's thumb. That didn't sound like fun to Clayton.

But then again, that's why they called it work, right? It wasn't supposed to be fun. And yet, all the advice he had received throughout his youth had emphasized that if you could do something you love for a living, you would never work a day in your life. You would just get up and have fun everyday. He wondered if people just said that to shut kids up. Maybe he needed to think about what he enjoyed doing.

After dinner, he raided the little refrigerator in his room for a Pepsi. He knew it would be expensive, but if he had to give up all his old habits just because he was temporarily out of funds, then life was hardly worth living.

His thoughts turned to Lulamae. She would be horrified to hear what he had in mind. In fact, she would be horrified to hear the way he was thinking in general. She had provided Clayton and his siblings with a moral compass at a time when his father was too preoccupied with his wife's mental health to spare much time for the kids. She was godmother to all the Masters and Garrisons of his generation, but she had been deeply involved with his upbringing and that of his siblings. Probably because she'd been so close to his mother.

He popped open the Pepsi he'd taken out of the refrigerator and took a drink. Maybe he should touch base with Austin before he did anything else. His brother had lived in Eagle's Toe for over a year now. Surely, he would be able to provide the name of a local lawyer.

He took a long drink and drained the can. Having a plan filled him with energy. Of course, the Pepsi's sugar probably helped, too. He gravitated to the window again, trying to get his bearings. He had GPS in the car, but he always wanted to know the lay of the land. Even the night before in that cramped little motel room, he had used the compass on his phone to figure out north and south. Before he could sleep, he needed to know which way pointed home. The October sun was setting, so he should be able to figure directions just by looking out the window.

By the time he retired for the evening, he was feeling a lot friendlier toward his environment. The bed was comfy, there were chocolates on his pillow, and he found a channel playing action movies. Somewhere in the middle of "Die Hard," his mind began suggesting he could find the woman he needed hanging from a bed sheet out the hotel window. Just as he was about to save her, she lost her grip and landed in the parking lot below. As she fell, her face transformed into the criminal who fell to his death at the end of the movie, only in Clayton's version, the body landed hard, smashing his father's Mercedes. He jerked awake, threw off the covers, and stumbled to the window.

No, the car was fine. He ran a hand through his hair and returned to the bed. Good grief, would his father consider his planned deception to be a crime? He turned off the TV and struggled to get comfortable in his bed of guilt.

Chapter Four

Monday

KENZIE WAS AMAZED AT HOW easily the farm chores came back to her. The one thing she'd forgotten was that a wise woman takes her shower after the barn chores, not before. At least her new job was at Taylor's Feed and Grain, so she hoped nobody would have a problem with the odors that clung to her. She climbed into her dad's old flatbed truck and turned the key.

For a moment, she thought it wasn't going to start. But at last, the engine coughed and sputtered and came to life. It didn't sound too healthy, but at least it was running. It had been a while since she drove a stick. However, this was the truck she learned to drive in so it wasn't difficult for her at all. She backed it up, turned it around, and groaned as the stick shift screeched from one gear to another. But she was in forward motion, and she was headed off for a new job and hopefully, a new life.

The flatbed ran steadily all the way to the Feed and Grain. Once there, Kenzie realized there was no room to park the truck in front of the store. She hoped that Mr. McAvoy wouldn't mind if she borrowed a spot in his lot. She turned into the Cattleman's parking lot and squeezed the truck into a space made for a much thinner vehicle. When she turned off the key she listened to the engine die and realized it was not a normal sound. Part of her wanted to pretend she hadn't noticed anything wrong. Part of her wanted to get out of that flatbed and head to the Feed and Grain and start her workday. But the realist in her forced her to turn the key to see if the engine would start again. Nothing. Whatever that flatbed had left, it had spent it getting her into town. If she wanted to get home again that afternoon, she was going to have to call someone to fix the truck. Nothing was going to be easy. That was becoming very clear.

She yanked the key out of the ignition, shoved the door open, and jumped to the ground without using the step. She remembered to reach back for her purse, then she slammed the truck door, glanced left and right for traffic, and jogged across the street to the Feed and Grain. She would have to call the garage first thing.

When she opened the door to the Feed and Grain, a bell tinkled overhead, and she looked up at the wall clock. Five minutes after ten. Not a great start. And of course with her luck, her new boss was already there and probably had been for several hours.

Taylor Garrison's voice came from somewhere amongst the shelving. "Kenzie? Is that you? Good morning." A moment later, her face appeared at the end of a row of flytraps. Kenzie tried to catch her breath as she hustled behind the counter and stowed her purse underneath the cash register.

"Good morning, Mrs. Garrison. Sorry I'm late. Not a good way to start my first day."

Taylor came up the aisle, wiping her hands on her jeans. "It's dusty back there," she said. "I'll have to talk to Cody about that. From the sound of your voice I would guess that you've already had a little drama this morning."

Kenzie did a double take. "Your hair is blue!"

Taylor ran a hand through her fresh bob. "The salon finally got my color in. You saw my natural pale blond when you interviewed. But this is the real me. When you're five feet tall, you have to do something to keep from being overlooked. Now, what happened to you this morning?"

Kenzie drooped all over as she confessed, "I took a few minutes to try and get the pig poop off my shoes, and then I discovered that my dad's flatbed truck has a top speed of forty miles an hour. On top of that, I think it just breathed its last in the Cattleman's parking lot. I hope you don't mind, but I have to call the garage and have someone come over and take care of that truck before I leave today at four." She glanced at the clock. "Sorry. Four-ten."

"Go ahead and call," said Taylor. "I keep the number for the Eagle's Toe Garage by the phone. Our delivery truck needs a lot of attention. When you're done, come back and find me, and I'll give you a tour of the stockroom."

"Thanks. I will."

After explaining her problem to the friendly fellow at the Eagle's Toe Garage, Kenzie went looking for Taylor and spotted her blue hair through the shelving. "You're right about the hair color. It makes you stand out."

Taylor smiled. "When I first came to town, everyone thought I was nuts for having blue hair. What's the story with the Garage?"

"Some guy named Brady said he would come over as soon as he could, but I shouldn't expect him before two o'clock. I hope he can jerry-rig something to get me home."

"Brady Felton can fix almost anything," said Taylor. She cocked her head to one side. "What happened to that red Mustang you were driving?"

Kenzie felt her color rising. She sent her gaze up and down the aisle, as if an answer might be waiting somewhere. At last, she mumbled, "Car trouble."

"It's not running either?"

"You could say that, yes."

Taylor put her hand on the stockroom door knob. "Hopefully, your luck will turn soon," she said. "Come on, I'll introduce you to Cody and show you the lay of the land."

♡

Clayton slept until noon. He didn't have anywhere to be, and he realized as he reached for his phone that he had set it to "do not disturb." There were three missed calls from his father, so in retrospect he decided he'd made the right decision. The temptation to turn over and go back to sleep was huge. But if he did that, he knew it would make him feel like the playboy loser his father said he was. That thought forced him out of bed.

He took a quick shower and got dressed. Because he had taken the Mercedes and gone to Colorado on impulse, he hadn't packed any clothing. He had to put on the same thing he'd arrived in, and he was beginning to worry that by doing so he had negated his shower. At the top of his list of things to do was find a place to pick up some clothing. Maybe his father was right. Maybe he was a total dingbat.

The text messages on his phone, however, told a different story. With his brother Dallas working for the family in China, Clayton had realized after leaving Latin America that he would need to travel even further if he wanted to see him. His visit to China had changed his life in a big way. His brother translated for him as they toured the country.

One of the things he found especially tragic was the number of orphans who were abandoned because their parents either could not afford them or already had as many children as the government would allow. Many of those babies were girls, who were being raised by foster families while waiting to be adopted. Some remained in orphanages, where resources were lacking. The plight of those children touched his heart. Before leaving China, he'd had his brother help him set up a special account so he could send funds to the orphanages nearest the family offices.

Ever since returning to the states, he had been sending a healthy portion of his monthly allowance to assist orphanages in China. With his brother working and living there, he knew that the use of his money would be overseen by Dallas. The text messages that had come in overnight included a thank you in broken English from the director of one of his beneficiary orphanages and three photographs of some of the children the money was helping. He had sworn his brother to secrecy. There was no point in explaining his charity to his father. It was better to let him think that Clayton regularly blew his monthly allotment on pretty girls and gambling in Las Vegas.

The irony of his recent trip to Las Vegas was that for once he actually had splurged and used some of his money to gamble. He'd kept telling himself that if he won, he could send a double donation to China. Unfortunately, no one told the casino or the roulette wheel of his plan. They did not care anything about children in China.

He had heard his father say hundreds of times over the course of his life that it was enough to take care of one's own. No one could help everyone in the world who needed it, and the Masters money was better used for business investments so that it could grow and increase and provide paying jobs for those less fortunate. Clayton would never call his father a tightwad, and Plano was certainly generous when it came to bonuses and gifts for those who worked for him. But Clayton knew in his heart that Plano would not understand the need he felt to send thousands of dollars a month to children he did not even know.

He sent a quick response to the manager of the orphanage and thanked her for the pictures. He couldn't help but smile every time he looked at them. There was also a text from his brother, filling him in on the various purchases that had been made with his donation.

After he finished attending to his text messages it was nearly one o'clock and he still had not figured out where he was going to buy a couple pairs of jeans and some T-shirts. He stopped at the front desk in the hotel lobby, where a jolly fellow with enormous eyebrows and a gap in his teeth directed him to head up the street on the east end of the parking lot and look for Mina's Boutique at the end of the block.

"No offense," he said, "but I was hoping to find a place that sounds a little more manly."

"Well, if you don't find what you need there, you can try the Feed and Grain across the street, but only if you're looking for farmer's overalls and sturdy boots." He reached across the counter to shake Clayton's hand. "I'm Reese McAvoy. I own the Cattleman's Inn. Your brother Austin is a fine young man. I hope the room is all right."

Clayton's arm was nearly bounced out of its socket, as McAvoy pumped his hand the whole time he was talking.

Clayton pulled his hand back as diplomatically as possible and used it to toss McAvoy a mock salute. "The room is excellent," he said, "and thanks for the information. I'll head straight down to the Boutique. Wish me luck."

McAvoy grinned and nodded, then picked up a phone and began punching numbers.

Clayton headed outside. The sun was doing its best to warm the October day, but a slight breeze coming off the mountains to the west made it feel colder than it looked. He shoved his hands in his pockets and strode up the street. By the time he reached Mina's Boutique, a motherly figure with a long gray braid and an ankle-length green plaid skirt was holding the door open.

"Hello! You must be Clayton. I'm Mina. Come on in."

"Is there a hidden network of surveillance cameras following my every move?"

"Nope. Just a phone line. Reese McAvoy is married to my cousin, Alice Kate." She beamed a multi-megawatt smile. "Lost your suitcase, eh?"

Clayton shrugged. It was as good a story as any. "You might say that." He stepped inside and his hopes faltered. "I'm not really the kind of guy who wears lace and heels."

Mina laughed. "In that case, you'll want to do your shopping in our men's department. Follow me."

The boutique was doing a brisk business, and the smell of fresh coffee and warm cookies made his mouth water.

Mina led him through a rough wooden door in the northwest corner of the shop, where the atmosphere changed completely. No lace or high heels here. "Now tell me," said Mina, "are you into trying things on, or do you know what sizes you wear?"

Half an hour later, Clayton was headed back to the hotel with an assortment of jeans, slacks, tees, shirts, and underwear. He made a note to come back for a jacket if it got any colder. Or maybe he'd try the Feed and Grain and see what the local males were decked out in.

Once in his room, he called down for a burger and fries, then changed out of his funky travel clothes and dressed from the skin out in clean boxers, new jeans, a navy tee, and a thick corduroy shirt. He'd forgotten socks and made a mental note to get new ones as soon as he could. Meanwhile, he slipped back into his running shoes—perfect for a man running away—and sat at the table by the window to eat his lunch. So far, so good. He was more or less incognito, even though his dad had made a few tries at reaching him by phone.

He was tempted to call him back just to see if he'd noticed the Mercedes was gone. Would he be furious? Angry enough to put a freeze on his allowance? Or maybe send some of his more talented detectives out on his trail?

His heart froze as he spotted a tow truck cruising the parking lot. Had his father noticed his switcheroo and somehow figured out where he'd gone? Was that tow truck driver looking for a black Mercedes? He burst out of his room and punched the call button for the elevator. When the doors did not open immediately, he pushed through the stairwell door and pounded down the concrete steps. He wasn't sure what he was going to do once he reached the parking lot, but he needed that car.

♡

It was two-thirty before Brady showed up with his tow truck. Kenzie caught sight of him through the front window of the Feed and Grain. "Mrs. Garrison? I need to run over and talk to the tow truck driver."

"We're practically the same age. Please call me Taylor."

"Thanks." Kenzie flashed a grim smile. "I won't be long."

"If he can't fix your truck by four, I'll ask Cody to drive you home."

That cheered Kenzie up a bit. She'd concentrated on learning the ins and outs of the retail feed and grain business and hadn't shared much with Taylor. But then, it was her first day, and she already had enough trouble, darn that old truck. No point in letting her new boss think she was a chatterbox. She grabbed her coat and shoved her arms in the sleeves on her way out the door.

Once she reached the parking lot, she waved at Brady. He must have come to Eagle's Toe after she went away to college because he didn't look familiar to her. But he was handsome as could be—she spotted the glint of a ring on his left hand— and yep, he was married.

She was almost close enough to speak to him when a brash and angry blond man nearly knocked her over in his haste to reach the door of the tow truck.

"Whatever they're paying you," he said, "I'll double it. Just pretend you didn't see it."

Brady cocked his head to one side. "Didn't see what?"

"That's the idea," said the Nordic negotiator. "Now how much?" He pulled out his wallet and started counting cash.

Kenzie gawked at the man. What nerve! He just butted in without giving her a glance. "Hey, Jerk Face. You nearly knocked me down."

"Sorry," he said brusquely, finally acknowledging her existence. Once he looked at her, he had to look again, and his eyes lingered for a moment. At last, he said, "Jerk Face is my father. My name's Clayton. My apologies, ma'am." He turned back to the tow truck driver. "Well? How much?"

Brady narrowed his eyes and thought for a moment. "Two hundred."

Clayton counted out twenties and handed them over. "They weren't paying you much."

Brady shrugged. "I didn't actually haul it away yet."

"Sounds fair," said Clayton. "Thanks a bunch." He gave Kenzie another look, one filled with interest and a tinge of regret, then hunched against the October breeze and headed back to the lobby of the Cattleman's Inn.

Kenzie's mouth hung open.

Brady got out of his cab and tipped his cap to her. "Hello. You must be Kenzie. You called about your dad's old flatbed, right?"

"Yes, that's right."

"I spotted it already. I've worked on it a few times before. You go on back to the Feed and Grain. When do you get off?"

"Four."

"Plenty of time. I'm Brady Felton. I inherited the garage from my uncle." He held out a hand and Kenzie shook it. "I'll work my magic on the flatbed right here in the lot. Key?"

Kenzie fished it out of her pocket. "That's real nice of you. Umm, if you don't mind, I'm going to need an estimate before you do much. This is my first day at work, so I'm short on cash."

Brady held the two hundred dollars aloft. "Don't worry. I think Mr. Jerk Face covered it." He winked at her.

"You know him?"

"Nope. Don't care to, either. But if he's giving away money, I'm happy to put it to good use. When you get home, give my regards to your folks. I'll leave the key on the seat. If anything really serious is wrong, I'll text you."

"Thank you, Brady. I really appreciate this." She gave him her cell number. "I'll be sure to tell my folks." She hummed a little tune as she crossed the street to Taylor's Feed and Grain. As she hung up her coat and returned to the cash register, she felt like her luck was improving. What a nice thing for Brady to do! Then she remembered her phone was turned off. She dug it out of her purse and powered it up. As soon as it was able, it pinged six times. She rolled her eyes. Todd. She glanced at the most recent text. Mentally, she edited out the expletives and name calling. It all boiled down to one question.

"Where is my car??!!!"

Chapter Five

CLAYTON RETURNED TO HIS hotel room, wishing he hadn't forked over two hundred dollars. He couldn't be sure that tow truck was actually looking for his dad's Mercedes, but better safe than sorry. He settled at the table to count his remaining funds. A little over four thousand remained in his money belt. Thank goodness Austin hadn't reserved a suite for him. He resisted the urge to raid the little refrigerator. No point in paying five bucks for a can of soda.

His musings were interrupted by a knock at the door. He had a wild thought that the tow truck guy had tracked him down because he'd gotten a better offer from his old man. Shaking his head in disgust at his own paranoia, he answered the door.

"Austin! Come on in."

Austin Masters was shorter than Clayton, wore his brown hair moussed to the sky, and blinked shyly through wire-rimmed glasses. His ever-present camera bag hung from one shoulder.

"Good to see you, Clay." He gave his brother a hug, which turned into an awkward grab and hold when Austin zigged and Clayton zagged.

Clayton laughed softly. "Same old clumsy Austin. How do you even keep your camera still when you're doing a shoot?"

Austin pushed his glasses up his nose and replied somberly, "Tripod."

"And what's with the glasses?"

"My contacts. Lost my contacts. Erin ordered new ones."

Clayton led the way to the little table. "Thanks for the room reservation, buddy. You know I'm good for it. Eventually. Speaking of Erin, where is the little bombshell?"

36

Austin settled his camera case on the foot of the bed and took the chair opposite Clayton. "I wanted us to have a few minutes in case we had brother stuff to talk about. Besides, she's teaching. I would have been here sooner, but she called me between classes to tell me about some gossip. One of the teachers is married to a security guard, and he spotted a wreck over in the old quarry that he swears wasn't there last week. Everybody talks to everybody in a small town. It's good for the photography business."

Clayton grinned.

Austin drummed his fingers on the table as a prelude, then jumped right in. "I thought you should know that Aunt Polly is in town, visiting the grandkids. Her grandkids. I don't have any yet."

Clayton nodded. "Thanks for the heads up. I was thinking of driving out to Thor's cabin this afternoon. Maybe I should wait."

Austin shook his head. "No point. Polly came for the holidays."

Clayton frowned. "It's October."

"She says Halloween is a holiday. She plans to stay until January."

"Uh-oh. That complicates things."

"Were you hoping to stay at the cabin? Because they built her a mother-in-law's quarters on the south edge of their property. She was complaining because it's so far to walk up to the main house. So they bought her a Polaris to drive around on." He laid his cell phone on the table. "Here's a picture. Not very good. Just a snapshot."

The mother-in-law quarters looked like a whole house to Clayton. "They made it match the cabin?"

Austin nodded. "Thor figures if the town council ever lets him start building his luxury housing, people will check out his place to gauge the quality."

"I'm impressed." Clayton sighed. "Well, at least we're partway through the month. My cash should last until the next bank deposit."

Austin tilted his head to one side. "Well, Thor and Ashley will have an empty guest room now, if you don't mind helping with the little ones. Every visit turns into a pre-school class." He laughed softly at his little joke. "Are you and Dad arguing about money again?"

"You guessed it, little brother."

"Just start investing it."

"I am," said Clayton. "In a way."

"Not a very profitable way, sounds like."

Clayton chewed his bottom lip. "That's why I haven't told Dad what I'm doing. He's into profit, big time. I don't think he'd approve."

"He says gambling is throwing your money away."

Clayton let it lie. He didn't want to burden Austin with the truth about where his money went. He trusted his baby brother, but he also knew his limits. Austin would try his best to keep a secret, and as a child, he never snitched. But as a man, his honesty could get in the way, and sometimes the truth managed to slip out of his mouth, usually when no one was expecting it. Clayton changed the subject.

"Hey, have you seen that gorgeous girl working over at the Feed and Grain? Lordy, she's a sight."

Austin shook his head. "Must be the Shanes' daughter, Kenzie. Erin talks to Taylor all the time, and she said word is that Kenzie was coming home to help her folks out. Their farm isn't doing very well, and I guess Kenzie sold some property in Denver before she moved home. Taylor told Erin she came to her interview in a classic Mustang, but today, she's driving an old clunker. She probably left her good car at home with her folks."

Clayton perked up. "No kidding? Good looks and money, too? Maybe I'll ask her out."

Austin made a clucking noise. "Be careful with that one. Erin says the Shanes are one of the oldest families in Eagle's Toe, and they have a lot of friends."

"Don't worry, I won't hurt anyone. Why does everyone think I'm such a cad with the ladies?"

Austin laughed briefly, cutting it off when Clayton didn't laugh along. "Sorry. Just save the playboy stuff for the big city. Erin and I want to live here a long time." He pushed his glasses up on his nose. "Sorry we don't have a guest room in our apartment."

Clayton chucked his brother on the shoulder. "No worries. I'll be fine. I need to talk to Aunt Polly about something anyway, so I suppose I should just head over there. And regardless of what you may have heard from Dad, I don't really mess up everything I'm involved in." He added silently, *I just can't tell him what I'm doing because he might pull my monthly deposit out from under me.*

♡

Kenzie found her duties less than challenging, but that was fine. It made her feel better about her hourly wage. Even so, she managed to mess up a couple of transactions while her mind was on Todd's threatening texts. Red-faced, she apologized profusely to Taylor.

"Don't worry about it," said Taylor. "First-day jitters." She patted Kenzie on the arm. "You can make up for it by coming in four inches shorter tomorrow."

It took Kenzie a moment to get the joke. "Oh," she said at last. "Sure thing. I'm sure I can find at least one person on the planet who wants to cut me off at the knees."

"It's after four," said Taylor. "You've more than made up for the few minutes you needed to deal with your truck. And here comes Sunny for the late afternoon shift. Have you two met?"

Sunny breezed through the door with a ten-pound papillon in the dog carrier strapped to her chest. Her blond hair was in a French braid. She looked dusty, as if she'd already worked a shift somewhere else. "Hi, Taylor! I'm here. Is this Kenzie?" She held out her hand. "I'm Sunny Finch. I mean, Felton. Still not used to using my husband's name."

Kenzie shook her hand. "Cute dog," she said. "Kind of small for working livestock."

Sunny smiled. "Peanut is my champion trick dog. And my 'heart dog.' It's like having a tiny soul mate with four paws."

Kenzie nodded. She tried to be polite, but her mind was leaping ahead to the truck, the chores awaiting her at home, and more rude texts from Todd. And she hadn't heard anything from Brady Felton yet.

As if reading her mind, Sunny said, "Brady got your truck running. He says it should get you home, but you'll have to baby it along. He thinks it's on its last legs."

Taylor offered, "Brady runs the garage and Sunny runs the animal rescue."

Sunny lifted Peanut out of his carrier and set him down. He immediately began his rounds, as if that were his assigned job.

Kenzie watched the little dog as she said feebly, "Guess a lot of new folks have moved to town since I left for college."

"A few," said Taylor. "But most of us are pretty nice. Don't worry, we all know your folks, and they are so proud of you." She beamed at Kenzie as if they were related.

Kenzie lifted her purse from behind the cashier's desk. All these mushy good feelings were making her nervous. Todd was only nice when he wanted something. She backed toward the door. "Nice to meet you, Sunny. I'll be back in the morning, Taylor." She turned and hotfooted it across the street.

She found a Post-It note on the steering wheel. "Baby this truck. Call if you need me. Brady." He'd left his number, too.

Her phone buzzed against her hip for the tenth time in an hour. She pulled it out, turned it off, and tossed it back in her purse. Then she got behind the wheel and began the intricate two-step involved in getting the motor to turn over. Once it caught, she took a breath to calm herself. She had known Todd would be upset when he discovered the Mustang was gone. She laughed at her own understatement. He was fit to be tied and probably wanted to wring her neck. Imagine how mad he'd be when he learned what she'd done to it. She hadn't yet got up the nerve to send the photo she'd taken of the Mustang's remains. Maybe tomorrow. She needed to get home so her dad wouldn't try to do all the evening chores alone. He looked so tired all the time. Had he looked that way when she was in high school? She couldn't remember.

She shifted into reverse and tapped the gas.

Someone honked urgently behind her. She stomped on the brake, forgot about the clutch, and the engine died. "No, no, no!!!" She begged the universe to make the truck start again, but no luck. A moment later, someone banged on the driver's door, and she nearly jumped out of her skin.

"You!"

"You!!"

They made their accusations at the same time. The last thing she needed was another confrontation with Jerk Face. She shoved the door open, hoping it would knock him on his behind, but he managed to get out of the way in time.

"What do you want?" she snapped. "You scared me into stalling my engine."

"Well, you scared the heck out of me, too. You nearly backed up into my dad's Mercedes. My Mercedes. Mine."

"Okay, okay," said Kenzie. "I get it. It's your car. Possession is nine-tenths of the law. Now get out of my way. I have things to do." *Lots more important than staring at you, you big lug. Why do you have to look like a fresh-faced boy scout/movie star combo?* Aloud, she added, "Shoo!"

"How are you going to get anywhere in this old rust bucket? That engine didn't stall. It died. As in, bit the big one. Bought the farm. Know what I mean?"

Kenzie folded her arms and leaned against the side of the old truck. "Unfortunately, yes. I know exactly what you mean. Now I have to wait around for that dang tow truck again."

The boy scout reached out and pushed at the side of the truck with one finger, as if that would help it move. "This baby ain't going anywhere. You need a ride?"

"I'll figure something out," she snapped, but she already knew she had few options. Not even a cab, if her memory served. Maybe the garage still ran a cab service in town. She dreaded turning her phone back on.

The movie star shrugged and looked around, as if some parking lot pumpkin might turn into a golden coach. "Look, I'm sorry. I didn't mean to scare you. If you need a ride home or something, I'll take you. You look like something's on your mind."

Kenzie looked him hard in the eye. In those dazzling green eyes. Her gaze shifted to his beach-boy hair, blond and streaked with sunshine. He was certainly a looker. But she didn't need that right now. Another man was the last thing she needed, darn it. However, she did need a ride home. She should be safe. After all, this was Jerk Face. It shouldn't take much to resist any charm he might dig up from deep inside.

"Okay," she said. "I do need a ride." She grabbed her purse and slammed the heavy metal door. "Lead on."

"Clayton," he said. "My full name is Clayton Jerk Face Masters. Just something to file away for future reference."

Kenzie almost smiled. At least he had a sense of humor…and seemed devoid of hard feelings. She followed him behind the truck and let him hold the door of a very expensive-looking black car while she slid in. As he got behind the wheel, she cast a little shade on his evident prosperity. "Does your father know you stole his Mercedes?"

She nearly choked when he responded, "Does yours know you pushed your Mustang over a cliff?"

Chapter Six

CLAYTON EXPECTED A BARBED comeback. Instead, Kenzie fell darkly silent. After several uncomfortable seconds, Clayton said, "Um, hey, I was just teasing. My brother told me someone found a wreck at the old quarry. I didn't really mean to make it sound like an accusation."

Kenzie leaned back in her seat and took a deep breath. A moment later, she said evenly, "There are more things in this world than gossip. My father knows a lot of things because he believes a person should read the newspaper every morning. He deals in fact, not gossip. Did you know that American cod fishing is at an all-time low? That people in Maine are losing their family fishing boats because they can't bring in enough to make a decent living?"

Clayton took his eyes off the road long enough to spare her a sideways glance. At least she was talking again. "No," he said somberly, "I did not know that. Do you have relatives in Maine?"

"No, but I can still feel sympathy for people who are losing everything."

Clayton nodded. "I see your point. What happened to your car?"

"I don't own a car. I had to borrow one to get here." She turned and looked out the passenger window.

"Oh, I see. So you're driving your dad's truck because you had to give it back. Got it. Do I turn left or right here?"

"Left."

He pulled onto the two-lane. She was even more beautiful when her fire was up. Dark brown hair and eyes, two spots of hot pink on her cheeks, and a lean, lanky athletic build that made his blood race. He managed to check her ring finger. Empty.

"Are you single?" he asked, trying for an innocent question.

"Very." Bang. Down came the cone of silence again.

Clayton waited a full minute before he spoke. "I'm batting a thousand, aren't I? Is there anything I can say that won't make you wish I was dead?"

Kenzie looked surprised. "I don't wish you were dead." She shook her head. "Like you said before, I got a lot on my mind."

"Such as?"

"Such as figuring out how to kill the man I *do* wish was dead. Turn down that dirt road."

Clayton obliged. "Well, I guess I deserved that smart remark. Let me offer a peace pipe, okay? Since your truck isn't going anywhere for the foreseeable future, will you let me pick you up tomorrow morning and take you to work?"

Kenzie blinked at him as if she didn't know whether to accept or not.

Clayton smiled. "It's just a ride to work. Honest. No catches, no small print." He stopped the Mercedes about twenty feet from the front porch.

Kenzie nodded. "Nine-thirty? My shift starts at ten."

"I'll be here." He gave a mock salute.

Kenzie finally offered up a tiny smile as she exited the vehicle.

Clayton's heart soared as he backed the Mercedes up to turn around. His new mission in life was to see a full-blown smile on that gorgeous face.

♡

Kenzie's smile faded by the time she reached the front door. Her heart was pounding. How could they have spotted the Mustang so soon? Thank goodness she hadn't sent that photo to Todd. It would be proof that she had pushed the car over the edge.

But what about fingerprints? Would they bother to take fingerprints off the car?

Her breath tightened in her chest as she tried to think. Her own fingerprints were not on file anywhere, so they shouldn't be able to match hers to anyone. But Todd's? Well, they could trace the car back to him, probably, if they'd found it. Would he press charges?

She headed for the kitchen. Her mother was sitting at the table, staring out the kitchen window.

"Hi, Mom. I'll get my boots and overalls on and go help Dad. Is he mad that I'm late? His old truck gave up the ghost. I had to get a ride home." She stopped short when she realized her mother was still staring out the window. "Mom? Is everything okay?"

As if waking from a dream, her mother said, "Oh, hello dear. You'll have to do the chores by yourself this afternoon. Your father isn't feeling well."

Kenzie frowned. "Has he got a cold? Oh gosh, he didn't come down with the flu, did he?"

"No, no, nothing like that. Sometimes…sometimes he gets tired, all of a sudden like, and he needs to lie down."

"Well, what does the doctor say?"

"You know your father. He won't go to a doctor. He claims he would know if he were sick."

Kenzie lowered herself onto a chair. "Mom, that doesn't exactly sound healthy to me. Does it to you?"

Marigold lowered her gaze to her lap. "No, of course not. But I've talked until I'm blue in the face, and it just makes things worse." She looked Kenzie in the face, and her gaze strengthened. "It won't kill us to do the chores by ourselves now and then."

Kenzie knew her mother well enough to know she was worried sick about her father. But he was probably the most stubborn man on the planet.

"I think your dad is worried about money," she said. "We were hoping, when you close on your house sale, you might be able to lend us a bit."

Kenzie rubbed her hands on her jeans. "Sure. Of course. I just haven't seen any cash yet." *Liar, liar, pants on fire. How long can I go on with this deception?*

Marigold pushed herself up from the table. "I can lend you a hand," she said. "With the animals."

Kenzie touched her arm. "No worries, Mom. I'll do the chores. You rest a bit."

Marigold nodded. "Perhaps I will. Is soup all right for dinner?"

"Soup is fine," said Kenzie. "I'll go feed the animals." She watched as her mother trudged toward the stove. Had her parents aged that much in four years? She wanted to tell her mother what was going on—about Todd, about the car, about all the lies and her troubles with money—but no way could she lay that burden at Marigold's feet today.

The barn smells were comforting and helped calm Kenzie's anxiety about the possible discovery of the car, but now she had even more to weigh her down. Her father was sick. She was sure of it. He never took a nap during the day. He never admitted he was tired. And now her mother had confessed that they were counting on her for financial help. She fed the goats and the chickens, then moved on to the pigs. Her folks only had two sows left. When she was in high school, they had sixteen, and every year, they sold piglets to Four-H kids.

The whole time she was away at school, they never said a word about money trouble. She had worked full-time to pay her way, so she hadn't come home for summer vacations. For her, there were no vacations. But their phone calls and letters had made everything sound normal. Not that her parents were big on either phone calls or writing letters.

They must not have shared anything with her siblings, either. That made sense, though. Both her brothers were serving in the Marines and her sister was in the Navy, seeing the world, as she had put it when she enlisted.

Dinner with her mother was simple and silent. Kenzie felt like she should try to cheer up her mother about whatever was going on with her father, but she just didn't have any cheer to spare. None. Nada. Zip. Every time she thought of something to say, she bit it off because it all spiraled back to how upset she was about her own life. Better to say nothing. Her mother was having a bad enough day already.

"How's the soup?" asked Marigold.

"Good. Fine." Kenzie forced a brief smile.

Marigold's gaze would shift upward in the direction of the bedroom where John lay in bed. Then she'd catch herself doing it, and jerk her eyes back to her bowl.

"Homemade," she said. "Got it out of the freezer," she added as if in apology. "I've been so worried about your father."

Kenzie nodded and sipped a spoonful of soup. "Is he eating?"

"I took up a tray."

"Okay." Kenzie scrambled for something safe to talk about. "Oh, you might like to know that everyone in town thinks you and Dad are wonderful."

Marigold looked surprised. "Really?"

"Yes. Even the new people. There seems to be quite a few new faces in town."

"The place really perked up when Kevin Fineman Wake brought his bride back to the Rocking Eagle," said Marigold, staring at her soup. "I think his mother wants him to run for office."

"Yes, you mentioned that once already. I remember Kevin! And his kooky sister, Karla. Does she still dress up as a vampire?"

Marigold smiled. "No, she seems to have moved on from that. Bringing the family back to Eagle's Toe was a real smart move on Krystal's part."

"You two were close in school, weren't you?"

"High school. We sure were." She shook her head. "That feels like a million years ago."

"To me, too," said Kenzie. "I mean, my high school days."

"She used to come over here to ride on our trails on weekends. So sad, the way her family pushed her to marry that stockbroker fellow. Didn't turn out so well, did it? But I think she's happy now." Her tone hushed. "She got a divorce and married her true love. She had him working as her ranch foreman."

Kenzie was touched. "That is so sweet. It's nice to know that sometimes things can work out for the best."

Marigold pinned Kenzie with a questioning gaze, but a thump from upstairs deterred her from asking what she wanted to know. Instead she got up and hurried to the stairs. "John?! You okay?"

Kenzie heard a muted reply. It sounded like her Dad was back to his grumpy self.

Marigold returned to the table and sat down. She twisted her napkin in her hands. "He said he's feeling better, but he's going to stay in bed this evening. Said he'll be okay in the morning."

"Good," said Kenzie. "That's a relief." She shook her head. "I don't remember Dad ever being sick before."

"Well, we're all fine until we're not, aren't we?"

"Wow, Mom, that's deep," teased Kenzie.

Marigold was obviously relieved that John was feeling better. She seemed to relax enough to sop up soup with her bread. "Oh, sweetheart, I haven't asked how your first day at work went."

"It was fine. I like Taylor. It's nice to be doing something other than waitressing."

Marigold frowned. "I don't understand."

Kenzie stumbled over her words. "I mean, in Denver, I was working anywhere I could, and evidently I'm a really good waitress. Not exactly what I went to college for."

"Don't worry. All young people have to start at the bottom."

Kenzie shrugged. "I guess. Although Clayton—the fellow who offered me a ride to work tomorrow—seems to have started out at a whole different level."

"Nice of him to help you out. You think the old truck is done for?"

Kenzie's expression contorted in pain. She hated adding more bad news to her mother's burden. "Brady thinks it has breathed its last. It's sitting in the Cattleman's parking lot."

Marigold shrank in her chair. "Oh, dear."

Kenzie dunked a piece of bread in her soup. "No worries. Dad can drive the Ford, right?" Her father had parked his more modern pickup next to the barn.

Her mother's hands began to tremble, and she shoved them into her lap. "The Ford needs a new transmission."

"Uh-oh. He didn't tell me."

Marigold took a deep breath and let it out in a flood of information. "We were really hoping you could help us out, now that you've sold the house," she said. "Getting a functioning vehicle is at the top of the list. And there's painting the house and maybe putting in a garden in the spring. Fact is, your father hasn't been able to do much for a couple of years now. And there are pushy folks out there trying to talk us into fracking on the property. And John was desperately hoping you could help us turn things around."

"I'll do everything I can, Mom. There's nothing left for me back in Denver. I feel like I wasted a whole year of my life."

Mom reached for her hand. "I'm so sorry. I know you were in love with Todd."

Kenzie made a face. "At least I know what they mean when they say love is blind. I only saw what I wanted to see."

"You'll feel a lot better when you get a big check for the house. I hope you don't mind if I ask you to use some of it to help us get a vehicle."

Kenzie set her spoon down. The deceit she'd been perpetrating on her parents churned within her. She would have to keep up appearances a while longer. She couldn't tell her parents what had really happened in Denver. Not with her father falling ill. And even though her mother seemed okay physically, Kenzie feared that she might expire from disappointment if she knew the truth. So she forced a tight smile and lied to her mother's face. "Once I get that check, I'm going to put the whole thing in your checking account, Mom. So you tell Dad not to worry, okay?" *Because I'm doing enough worrying for all three of us.*

Chapter Seven

CLAYTON KNEW HE SHOULD stay on the highway and head west for his cousin's house. But his mind was full of Kenzie and how much she stirred his blood. Crazy the way things worked out. He came here thinking he might find a fake bride and pull a fast one on his father. Now all he could think about was this spitfire of a girl. Woman. This stunning, puzzling woman with the incredible sadness in her eyes. What could be so terrible at her age? She couldn't be more than twenty-four. And from an old Eagle's Toe family, to boot. Not wealthy, but they had roots in the land. That should impress his dad. Not like some roadside café waitress.

Then he shook his head. No, he couldn't pull Kenzie into a plan to fool his dad. When his father met Kenzie, Clayton wanted it to be under the best circumstances possible. He wondered who the villain was in Denver, the one she wished was dead.

He pulled into a little burger joint called The Nest. It looked like a time machine had picked up a 1950s drive-in and set it down on the edge of town, all shiny and new. It made him smile. He had to eat, and that would give him time to figure out what to do.

He gave his order to a perky youngster on roller skates. Outdoor speakers were playing old rock-n-roll, and when the Beach Boys finished urging him to be true to his school, a radio announcer broke in.

"You're listening to station KTOE, the voice of Eagle's Toe. All oldies, all the time. If you want modern music, find a younger disc jockey. But before we get to our next selection, I want to remind you all that Thor Security can handle all your home and business security needs. If you're worried about your family's safety, Thor Garrison will set you up with cutting-edge home security systems. Drop in and see him. He's located just half a block east of the Cattleman's Inn. And while you're in the neighborhood, stop on by the Il Vaccaro restaurant for a delicious Italian meal, or grab a snack at the Itty Bitty cafe, just a few doors down from Thor Security. That's Thor Security. If you love your family, you want to keep them secure.

"Ah, yes, love, love, love. And here's Elvis, telling us all about it."

"Love Me Tender" floated out of the speakers as the young waitress delivered Clayton's burger and milkshake. He paid her and gave her a five-dollar tip. The food was delicious. He sighed with contentment and leaned back in the driver's seat, thinking about his cousin. Thor had been a firefighter back in Texas. Clayton was a little foggy regarding the tragedy that sent Thor packing off to Colorado, but things had certainly turned out well for him.

Thor Security. He must know a ton about surveillance and all that jazz. Clayton wondered if his cousin had the skills to find out what had happened to Kenzie in Denver. Should he even ask? Maybe he should wait for her to reveal whatever it was in her own good time.

Then again, if he knew what was wrong, he might be able to help her out, make her feel better. And earn that smile he longed to see.

By the time he finished his burger, he knew he had to go to Thor's place. No point in putting it off. Besides, eventually he wanted to ask Polly about Lulamae. Maybe he should soften her up first.

He got out of the car and went inside The Nest. A white-haired gentleman behind the counter was wiping his hands on a bright red apron.

"Problem with the food?" he asked.

"No, sir. Best burger I ever ate. So good, in fact, I thought I'd take some along and surprise my cousin with dinner. Four cheeseburgers, four orders of fries, and four chocolate milkshakes, please."

Ten minutes later, he was stacking white take-out bags on the passenger seat of the Mercedes. Maybe small town living wasn't so bad after all.

Austin had drawn him a map of how to get to Thor's cabin. Clayton would have felt more secure with an address he could program into the GPS, but Austin confessed he didn't know the address. He'd never had to mail them anything. He just went in person.

That was so "Austin."

So Clayton drove slowly, checking the little hand-drawn map as he went. Austin had done a good job. He arrived while the milkshakes were still firm. He admired the landscaping and the dramatic statement the so-called cabin made, a large luxury home surrounded by stately pines and carefully planned flowerbeds, though little color remained at this time of year, except for greens and the dark mottled grays of tree trunks.

Clayton didn't know if Thor and his family were expecting him because Austin's conversations wound around so many corners, he wasn't sure if his brother had called ahead on his behalf or if he thought it was a bad idea. But any desire to change his mind and turn around was squelched when Rocky, the Doberman, bounded around the corner of the house and planted his front feet on the passenger side window, barking furiously.

Clayton remembered that his Aunt Polly used to raise Dobermans. But now she was downsizing to Chihuahuas, as evidenced by the little dog with the shrapnel bark that bounced high enough to be seen from the driver's side. Bounce, bark, drop. Bounce, bark, drop.

The dogs were soon followed by Ashley Garrison and a toddler, who ran by pumping his chubby arms while his legs maintained the only gait he had mastered thus far, a clumsy shamble. Ashley carried a baby on her hip. Clayton supposed it must be the little girl born…last year? The year before? He should have asked Austin for a summary of the family members when he had the chance.

Just then, his Aunt Polly drove around the house on a shiny new green Polaris. Two other Chihuahuas balanced for their lives on her lap, trying not to be thrown from the vehicle by Polly's impetuous fits and starts.

The Polaris died as she approached the Mercedes. She got out as if that's where she intended to park and peered through the driver's side window, staring directly at him.

"Well, I'll be. It's Clayton Masters, as I live and breathe." When she approached the car, the dogs renewed their hysteria. Her white-blond hair was fighting to free itself from a scrunchy. "Hush, all of you! You'll get some, whatever it is." She pulled the front door open before Clayton could kill the engine. "Is that burgers and fries I smell?"

"Hello, Aunt Polly." Clayton got out and hugged her. His affection was not appreciated by the Doberman.

Polly snapped, "Sit! Stay!"

Like magic, the big dog did her bidding, its nose twitching in the air as a long string of drool fell slowly to the ground.

Clayton was relieved. "I knew I brought an extra burger for someone," he joked. "I just thought it would be Thor."

Ashley stepped forward and extended her hand. "I think we met last summer, Clayton, when Thor and I took the children to visit Polly's ranch."

"Yes," said Clayton. "I doubt anyone forgets you once they've been introduced," said Clayton sweetly. "Your intelligence and beauty compete with the sun for brilliance." He knew it was corny, but he'd heard his father talk like that for years, and it just popped out.

Ashley smiled. "Oh yes," she commented, "the one with the silver tongue. Thor should be here soon. Come on in and make yourself at home."

The toddler mimicked his grandmother's "Sit! Stay!" and wagged a stern finger at the Doberman. "Fwies! I smell fwies!"

"That's enough, Odin. This is your father's cousin Clayton. And I'm sure he will share his fries with you."

"Sharp nose on that young man," said Clayton. "I'll bring the take-out bags."

"No, no," said Polly. "I'll do it. I'm not sure Rocky can resist robbing a stranger but he'll behave for me." She was obviously taking charge, so Clayton closed the driver's door and joined Ashley at the front door.

He said softly, "I'd forgotten how much…energy… she has."

Ashley laughed. "Tell me about it." She opened the door wide. "Please come in. It's so good to see you again." She led the way through the soaring living room. A playpen sat in one corner and the floor was strewn with toys "Let's settle in the kitchen. Otherwise we'll be fighting off canines while we eat."

A sleek and sassy American shorthair sunned itself in the window over the sink. The last rays were just visible over the treetops.

"Is it sunset already?" asked Clayton.

"Here among the trees, we lose the light early," said Ashley. She set the baby girl in a high chair. "May I offer you something? Coffee? It's the least I can do for the man who saved me from preparing dinner."

"Coffee would be fine," said Clayton. He stood back against the counter and watched Polly, Odin, and the dogs parade into the room.

Polly set the bags on the table as Ashley made coffee. She began pulling hamburgers and French fries out of the sacks. When she got to the milkshakes, her eyes lit up.

"Oh Clayton, you remembered my favorite. Chocolate milkshakes. Is this a bribe? Because if it is, it's working." She pulled the lid off one and dipped into it with a spoon. Her expression betrayed how much she loved ice cream. When she could talk, she said, "All right. I wasn't supposed to let on, but this milkshake has loosened my tongue." She lifted Odin to her hip and gave him a spoonful of milkshake.

"Let on about what?" asked Clayton, surprised at how comfortable he was in his cousin's kitchen with all its family hubbub.

"Plano called here about an hour ago."

Clayton froze. "He did, did he?"

"Seems he's missing his oldest boy and wanted to know if I'd seen you lately."

Clayton eased himself onto a kitchen chair and leaned back to allow the chubby gray cat to leap onto his lap. "And what did you tell him?"

"Well, I hadn't seen you yet, so I told him no." She moaned around another mouthful of milkshake.

"And you weren't supposed to tell me he called?"

Polly shook her head. "Nope. I'm not supposed to tell you he knows you took the Mercedes."

"Was he angry? I mean, angrier than usual?" asked Clayton.

"No, not really. He's trying to decide what to do next."

"Aunt Polly, you're going to make me beg, aren't you?"

Polly's eyes twinkled. She lifted her milkshake. "Nonsense. You brought me a little bit of heaven. I don't want to make you suffer." She gave Odin another spoonful.

Clayton stroked the cat and counted silently to ten. Rushing Polly just made her more stubborn. He knew she was dying to tell him something.

At last, Polly said, "Plano had a couple of visitors this morning. Couple of burly entrepreneurs, so to speak, out to repossess a fancy car. They said the owner was behind in his payments and they wondered if he was at home today."

Clayton closed his eyes and groaned. Internally, he was congratulating himself for getting out of Texas when he did.

"Of course, you weren't, and Plano sent them packing. So you can relax. But it piqued his curiosity and made him check the garage."

"Oh great."

Ashley set a cup of coffee in front of him.

"Thank you, Ash." He eyed his aunt. "Was that all?"

Polly shook her head. "He's trying to decide whether to call them burly boys back again. Seems someone left a Maserati in his garage." She tilted her head and smiled knowingly at him.

Rocky heard it first, the sound of a car approaching. He began bouncing and barking and ran to the front door.

Little Odin waved his arms and squealed, "Daddy! Daddy!"

Polly set him down so he could greet his father. Ashley smiled at Clayton and promised, "That's Thor. We'll be right back."

Clayton chuckled to himself. She sounded like a woman who had been left alone with Polly before and knew exactly what he was going through.

As soon as Ashley left the room, Polly leaned close to Clayton and used a stage whisper to add, "One more thing. Plano told me not to say a word about Lulamae."

Chapter Eight

Tuesday

THE NEXT MORNING, KENZIE rose an hour earlier than usual to allow enough time for doing all the chores by herself. Her father was still not up to it. But he did come down to breakfast, looking tired and wan.

Her mother was bubbling over with relief and cheer at having John hungry for breakfast, but Kenzie noted that she served him tiny amounts of food. He only ate half of that, and when he pushed the plate away, Marigold carried it to the sink and refilled his coffee cup without saying a word about it.

John spent a lot of time staring at Kenzie. She couldn't quite place his expression. It was new to her. As she prepared to leave the table, her dad's eyes misted over, and Kenzie realized with guilty horror that his expression was one of gratitude. That rattled her almost as much as the texts that Todd was still sending.

All in all, it had been an unsettling morning. She agonized again over the little deceits…big lies?…that she'd told them about Denver. Here she was, needing their support at the worst time in her life, and there they were, on the other side of the table, in desperate need of her assistance.

It was a relief to kiss them goodbye and step out on the porch to wait for Clayton. And bless his heart, he was right on time.

She left the porch and opened her own car door. "Good morning." She gave him a tiny smile.

"You look amazing," said Clayton.

"Thank you. This time I remembered to shower *after* I did the chores. You look terrible. Sleepless night?"

Clayton shook his head. "Visited relatives until two in the morning."

"Oh." She stretched the word into a very knowing singsong, up and down the scale. His hair was damp and combed straight back. He smelled delightful...not a hint of motorcycle oil or car grease...and except for the dark circles under his eyes, she had to admit that he didn't really look terrible. In fact, he looked darn good. Maybe it was the car. Would he look this good on a tractor?

She blurted, "Have you ever driven a tractor?"

Clayton pretended to pound water out of his ear. "Say again? I'm not sure I heard you right."

Kenzie suppressed a smile. "Have you ever driven a tractor?"

"Hmmm. That's what I thought you said. No, I'm afraid not. Should I learn?"

Kenzie shrugged. "It wouldn't hurt."

Clayton kept his eyes on the road, but his tone was light and welcoming. "How are your parents doing?"

Kenzie shrank into her seat. "My dad isn't feeling so great." She shook her head. "When I left for college, they were hale and hearty. Five years later, it's like all the life drained out of them. Well, out of my dad. My mom still has steel in her spine when she needs it."

Clayton made a sympathetic noise. "Family."

"Exactly." Kenzie wondered if she should be sharing all this with a man she barely knew, but he was easy to talk to. "What about your folks?"

"Oh, well, just my dad left. And my siblings. Do you know Austin Photography?" He pointed at a small storefront as they passed. "That's my kid brother."

"Was he the one you were up all hours with?"

"No. I was at my cousin's house. Thor Garrison? He's my cousin on his mother's side."

"Oh, yeah. He put in some security lights for my folks."

"Funny," said Clayton, pulling up to the curb of the Feed and Grain. "Thor and I are the same age, but he's got a great wife and two adorable kids. I feel...unproductive."

Kenzie's hand was on the door handle. "By the way, have you heard any more gossip about the wreck at the quarry?" Her heart pounded as she asked the question. She hoped she sounded casual.

"Actually, Austin called Thor's place last night and told us the whole thing was a false alarm. Turns out the wreck the watchman spotted had been there for years but the wind blew off the tarp that used to cover it."

Kenzie felt like a huge weight had been lifted. "Well, that's good. I mean, I'm glad no one was hurt. You know." She stumbled over her words, getting out of the car. She thought she might float into the Feed and Grain.

Before she closed the car door, Clayton leaned toward her. "But the sheriff is going to take a look, just to be on the safe side, either today or tomorrow. Can I take you home after work?"

Kenzie's knees turned to jelly. "Yes, please," she mumbled.

"Great. See you at four." He drove away.

Kenzie turned and trudged toward the Feed and Grain. She felt like a death row inmate whose request for a pardon had been denied.

♡

Clayton wasn't sure what he'd said wrong, but whatever it was, it had knocked the breath out of Kenzie. What on Earth could be that terrifying? He decided it was time for a private chat with Thor.

He parked the Mercedes in the Cattleman's lot and walked to Thor Security. The brisk morning air carried a hint of moisture although for the moment only friendly white clouds floated lazily across the sky. He spied Thor through the glass front of his store. His cousin was lifting weights, concentrating on his reps. He was facing away from the window, so Clayton just watched for a few moments.

How strange that they could be so much alike and yet so different. Clayton was sure that Thor would have the same muscle development if all he did was lift his kids up and down during the day. Clayton had the same gene for muscle, but he had never been a fan of organized workouts. He preferred hiking, skiing, and swimming, anything that could pass for recreation.

He figured Thor had an inner drive that he lacked. He had more in common with Ulysses, whose laid-back attitude was more Clayton's style. Where the heck was Ulysses anyway? Thor would know. He entered the store.

The bell over the door tinkled and Thor responded by reluctantly setting his barbell aside.

"Oh Clayton! Come on in. I was just getting in some reps. Have a seat." He indicated a wingback chair on the client side of his desk.

Rocky was sleeping on his bed in the corner. He barely lifted his head in greeting. They were old friends now. Clayton had fed the dog so many French fries and Milk Bone biscuits, Rocky had actually turned his head away and stretched out under the kitchen table somewhere around midnight. Now when he lifted his head long enough for a glance at the visitor, Clayton could swear it was the doggy equivalent of a guy with a hangover saying, "Yo, bro."

He grinned at his own mental image.

Thor took the chair behind the desk and leaned back on two legs. "What's up? You didn't get enough of Thor World last night?" His eyes sparkled.

Clayton crossed an ankle over his knee. "You have a great family. Ashley is amazing. How does she juggle all of that?"

"She runs a business, too. She and Mina from the Boutique are partners in the art gallery next door."

"No way!"

"Way." Thor let his chair drop to four legs. "Coffee?"

"Sure. Thanks."

Thor poured for both of them and confessed, "She also has a nanny and an employee or two at the gallery. And we have a housekeeper who comes three times a week."

Clayton took the offered coffee. "Well, thank God. The thought of her trying to do all of that and keeping you happy besides was too much to get my mind around." He sipped coffee.

Thor settled on his chair again. "And thanks to you, my dog is in a coma."

"You're welcome," quipped Clayton. "Aunt Polly sure bowed out early."

"She probably figured if you started feeding the Chihuahuas, they'd explode. Besides, she and Ashley enjoy having their own space."

Clayton lifted a knowing brow. "Nice little place you built for her."

Thor nodded. "She loves being near the grandkids. She just doesn't want to actually help out in any meaningful way." He put a finger to his lips. "Please don't tell her I said that."

Clayton chuckled. "No worries. Where is Ulysses? I thought he had a place here, too."

"He does. He and Belle are in Vegas, visiting Lulamae. Belle adores her."

"They have any kids yet?"

"Belle can't, so they're working on adoption."

"Cool." Clayton shook his head slowly. "Your babies are sure cute. I mean, once you get past the shriek factor."

"Sounds of life and joy," said Thor. "But um, that's why we have a nanny." He looked slightly uncomfortable. "And that's why I can't offer you a place to stay. She lives in."

Clayton brushed it away. "No worries. I'm staying at the Cattleman's. Turns out the owner is giving Austin a special price." He looked around. "Nice place. Lots of wall displays. An information video. Do you get much foot traffic?"

"Mostly by appointment," said Thor. "But a guy needs to go to work. If you get my drift."

"Speaking of which," said Clayton, shifting from family mode to the reason he'd stopped by, "I was wondering if you could help me out with something."

An hour later, Clayton emerged from Thor Security with great faith that his cousin knew more about security than just installing alarm systems. He was impressed. In fact, before he left, Thor had already made a phone call—Clayton didn't know who could provide an answer that fast—and discovered that Mackenzie Shane had never owned property in Denver, and she'd never registered a car in the state of Colorado.

Chapter Nine

WEDNESDAY AND THURSDAY, Kenzie found herself becoming more and more accustomed to riding in Clayton's Mercedes. Okay, his father's Mercedes. But that didn't matter to her.

He started bringing her little gifts. On Wednesday, it was hot coffee and croissants for the drive to work, and a sweet little cowgirl figurine on her way home. He had blushed and confessed, "She's dressed just like you. Except for the cowboy hat. I couldn't resist."

Kenzie found herself being more and more charmed by Clayton.

On Thursday morning, he brought coffee and donuts from The Muffin Man, and he offered to help her paint her parents' house.

"That would be wonderful." Gratitude filled her voice. "You wouldn't mind? I mean, don't you have a job to get back to? Am I going to come out some morning and discover you've headed back to Texas?"

He lifted a pastry and shook his head. "Once you discover The Muffin Man, there's no going back to Texas. And painting seems like an obvious way to help."

Thursday afternoon, he brought her a porcelain horse. "Your little cowgirl needs a ride. Do you like it?"

The figurine was the perfect size for the porcelain cowgirl. The horse was a pinto, black and white, with an arched neck and a fancy set of tack molded in great detail. "Oh my gosh, I love it." On impulse, she leaned over and planted a kiss on his cheek. Then she said, "Sorry. I have no right to do that."

"Sure, you do. I hereby give you blanket permission to kiss me any time you want."

Kenzie had tucked the little figurines under her pillow that night, and her dreams had been so sweet. She was a tiny cowgirl riding her porcelain pinto all around her bedroom.

Friday morning, Kenzie seriously considered smashing her cell phone with a hammer. If she wasn't still paying the monthly bill, she would have done it. She calculated that she would get a weeks salary from Taylor just in time to pay the bill. She was feeding the pigs when she realized her phone bill was going to the empty house in Denver. She sat down heavily on a bale of hay. The thought of calling the company and changing her address felt overwhelming. It was just one too many things to deal with.

She still hadn't heard anything about the sheriff checking out the quarry. A watchman might make a mistake, but she feared that a lawman would take a very close and thorough look at every inch of that quarry. And the threat of the Mustang being discovered hung darkly over her head. It filled her with gloom, and she moved among the barn animals without her usual banter.

Her phone was almost useless to her. She was afraid to read Todd's texts, and yet she felt compelled to do so. What if he reported the car stolen? He might not know exactly where her family lived—he wasn't the kind of guy you took home to meet Mom and Dad—but any competent police force would have her location pinpointed in a heartbeat. Every time her parents' phone rang, she would jump out of her skin and hold her breath until her mom greeted the person on the other end. Then and only then could she breathe easy. So far there had been no calls from police or the sheriff's office. But with every passing day, she grew more and more anxious about it.

In Todd's text of the night before, he had threatened suicide if she didn't tell him where to find the car. She still hadn't sent him a picture of the destruction.

At first, his threat set off all kinds of deep feelings inside. Sympathy, worry, guilt, and even a shadow of the affection she'd felt for him when they first met.

But she shook them off. After all, he had threatened suicide before. The first time, six months ago, she had treated him with kid gloves and promised to stop asking about the mortgage for the house.

The second time, three months later, she realized he was using his threats as a tool. If he really felt suicidal, he was perfectly capable of acting on that impulse. He could swerve his motorcycle into oncoming traffic or slit his wrists with the Bowie knife he carried hidden in his boot. Even so, he'd been extremely upset about something, so when he insisted they go on a road trip for a few days, she had agreed. She didn't even question him when he packed all their clothes into the Mustang. The car could barely run at that point in time, and the hood was a different color because he'd had to replace it. The weird thing was, they didn't go anywhere. At first, he said they would go camping in the mountains. But they had no equipment. They spent their nights in an isolated cabin in the woods. He claimed it belonged to one of his "associates."

Three days later, she informed him that she would lose her job if she didn't get back when she'd promised. So they went back to Denver. She literally got out of the car and had to change for work in the restaurant bathroom. She dropped three different orders that day because she was so distracted and nearly got fired anyway.

When he picked her up from work—he usually let her walk home, so that was suspicious, too—he was all smiles and had groceries in the trunk. He announced it was time to go back home.

That episode had raised so many questions in her mind. She should have left that very day.

But she didn't want to tell her parents her life was a sham. And there was still a flicker of the original fire she'd felt for Todd burning inside. So she stayed.

Emma the pig nudged her with a dirty snout.

"That's all there is, Emma. Just piggy kibble today. Mom has been too worried about Dad to do much cooking."

Marigold kept a bowl on the counter as she cooked, and into it went vegetable peelings and leftovers and an occasional Fig Newton for the pigs, to supplement their commercial pig chow.

"Maybe there's something left in the garden," said Kenzie. "I'll check after work, okay?" She stroked the pig's head, its sparse hairs bending like wire beneath her palm.

As she showered and dressed for work, she wondered if she had enough change in the bottom of her purse to buy Emma a package of Fig Newtons.

Then she had a great idea. On her break, she would stop in at the Itty Bitty cafe and see if Mrs. McAvoy would save some kitchen scraps for her pigs. Her plan filled her with purpose and she clung to it as she said goodbye to her folks. Her dad was still unable to help with chores, but he did seem to look a little better. Her mother, however, looked more worn and haggard every day.

That's what worry does, she thought as she stood on the porch waiting for Clayton. *I wonder how long it'll be before I start looking like that.*

Right on time, the black Mercedes pulled up in front of the house. The sight of it lifted her spirits. Clayton was turning out to be such a wonderful person. And he was so darned cute. Well, handsome really. But he knew how to turn on the boyish charm. He seemed really interested in her. She pretended she hadn't noticed, but he had been flirting like mad on their drives to and from the Feed and Grain. Maybe she could share some of her worries with him.

♡

"Good morning," said Clayton cheerfully. It earned him a fleeting smile. "How is your dad today?"

"Still resting." She tilted her head and teased, "Are you still unemployed?"

"I'm sort of on vacation." He let his hand waffle in the air. "Right now, I'm the chauffeur for a fantastic woman."

"Oh? Who?"

Clayton laughed. "You, silly."

"Ah. The 'fantastic' part threw me. I'm not feeling so awesome recently." She clutched her purse as her phone dinged.

"Is that for you?"

Kenzie seemed to cringe as she reached for her phone. She glanced at it, then shoved it back in her purse. "It's probably spam or a sales call."

Clayton wondered if he should tell her that he knew her life in Denver was nothing like she'd let on. He decided instead to offer advice.

"You can block unwanted callers."

She nodded. "Yeah, I know. But I need to keep tabs on him." She looked puzzled. "He keeps texting threats, but he never acts on them. Not a word about calling the police. He just seems to get increasingly frantic." She chewed her bottom lip. "Lately he's begun using the word 'please' a lot. He never once said 'please' to me when we were together." She stared into her lap. "Meanwhile, I'm afraid to turn the phone off because Mom might need me."

Clayton wished her ex would disappear off the planet. "Look, Kenzie…. I like you. A lot."

She smiled like Mona Lisa. "I figured. Why else would you be driving me to work and back home every day? And buying me adorable little gifts?"

Clayton slowed down for a cow in the middle of the road. "Gee, those signs aren't kidding." He nodded at the "Watch for livestock" warning by the edge of the road. He glanced sideways at Kenzie and let his eyes linger. She was gorgeous and didn't seem to know it. How many women looked good in jeans and a flannel shirt? He returned to his original thought. "Am I wasting my time? I mean, you're on the rebound. Maybe I should just drive and keep my feelings to myself for six months."

Kenzie looked at him, eyes wide. "After tempting me with priceless statuary? I called you Jerk Face and here you are buying me gifts." Her tone lightened. "By the way, I give you blanket permission to buy me little gifts any time."

Clayton smiled at the way she had turned his phrase around. "I brought coffee and muffins today. As for the Jerk Face thing"—he shrugged—"I've been called worse. And I've been known to irritate people from time to time."

The cow finally plodded off the highway, and Clayton eased the Mercedes forward.

He could feel Kenzie's eyes on him as he drove.

At last she said, "Whatever was supposed to be happening between me and Todd was over at least six months ago. I just stayed because.... I don't know. It was like I was paralyzed. Couldn't make a decision."

Clayton said, "Sounds like you might have been depressed."

Kenzie laughed sharply. "Oh God, that certainly fits." She leaned in his direction, a nice change from having her practically ride with one hand on the door, as if she were ready to jump out any second. She continued, "There is no rebound issue. There's definitely a 'How could I be so stupid' issue. Mixed in with a little bit of 'I wish Todd would drop dead.' But mostly it's me wondering why he hasn't reported his car stolen." She straightened up abruptly, as if she'd said too much.

Clayton played it cool. "Was that the car you 'borrowed' to get to Eagle's Toe?"

"Yep." She was staring out the window again.

Clayton pulled up to the curb in front of the Feed and Grain. "Hey, for what it's worth...."

She looked at him warily.

Clayton gave her his best little boy grin. "I've been known to make a bad decision here and there."

Something like gratitude flittered across her perfect face before she got out.

Clayton watched her move as she headed into the store. She had a natural grace that mesmerized him. Once she was inside, he drove off before lifting his phone to his ear.

"Hello, Thor? Here's another little detail that might help. But you didn't hear it from me. Her ex—first name Todd—had a classic Mustang that he might be looking for. Kenzie says she thinks it's strange that he hasn't reported it stolen."

Thor's voice sounded like he was on speakerphone. "Thanks. Now do me a favor and call Uncle Plano so he'll quit pestering Polly. She's driving us crazy with her complaints."

"Sure. Of course. Be glad to." Clayton hung up. "Rats."

Chapter Ten

KENZIE FOUND THE DISTRACTION of work a blessing. It left her little time to worry about her father or her ex. When one o'clock rolled around, she explained to Taylor that she needed to pop over to the Itty Bitty for a moment, and Taylor liked the sound of that so much, she handed her a twenty and asked her to pick up one of Mrs. McAvoy's pizzas for lunch.

"Make it a big one," she said. "There are three of us here at the moment."

"Thanks," said Kenzie, all too happy to let her three-day-old bread and its limp slice of American cheese rest in her purse all day. Emma would enjoy it.

At the Itty Bitty, Alice Kate McAvoy put their order in right away. Then she wanted to catch up with Kenzie.

"How are your parents doing? Reese and I have been concerned. They used to come over to the Cattleman's for dinner almost every week."

"I think they're a little short on funds right now," said Kenzie. "And my dad isn't feeling too great. Mom says it's probably the flu." She looked away to hide the little white lie. She changed the subject. "Mrs. McAvoy, can I ask a favor? Could you have one of your cooks save the vegetable ends and pieces for me? Fruit cores, lettuce ends, whatever? Mom has been too worried about Dad to keep up with her garden, and the pigs are feeling neglected."

"That's a lovely idea," said Alice Kate. "I feel so bad throwing out leftovers. You stop by on your way home and I'll have the first load for you." She shook her head sadly. "I was really hoping Marigold would have a surplus crop. Some of my patrons are very dedicated to eating local food grown without pesticides. When she's up to it, you might give her a little reminder."

"Sure. Will do."

"They are so lucky to have you move home when they need you most." Alice Kate's sympathetic gaze felt like laser burns to Kenzie. She shuffled her feet.

"I don't know how much help I really am," she demurred.

"Well, don't sell yourself short. You're here, you're working already, and I'm sure you're handling most of the farm chores." Alice Kate tipped her head to one side. "I hope I'm not being too nosy, but I thought when they took out that second mortgage they were going to use it to paint the house. And the barn, too, for that matter."

Kenzie was taken aback. Her mother hadn't mentioned any of that to her. A second mortgage? She thought the first one had been paid off years ago. Were they in that much financial trouble? Could they actually be in danger of losing the farm? What could have happened? The Shanes had been working that land for three generations. The thought of losing the farm made her stomach churn. She realized that Alice Kate was waiting for her to say something.

"I'm sorry, I was sort of out of that loop," she said lamely. "Do you happen to remember how long ago they took out that second?"

Alice Kate's eyes narrowed as she gazed into space, as if the past were being replayed on a big movie screen. "I'm thinking it was about two years ago," she said. Then her face lit up. "Oh! I know exactly when. It was right after Mr. Patterson was kicked by that cow and ended up in a wheelchair. So it was two years ago, maybe two and a half. Mrs. Patterson thought they were going to have to sell, but people got together and did a fundraiser for them, out at the Rocking Eagle. So they could stay on. And maybe pay some medical bills." She shook her head. "You know what a mess it is to get insurance these days. And it wouldn't surprise me a bit if poor Mr. Patterson had let his premiums lapse."

Kenzie processed Alice Kate's information. "He's selling his leather goods now," she said. "Taylor has him all set up to sell on-line. She says he's making good money at it, too."

Alice Kate looked relieved. "That's wonderful. I guess we all go through rough patches now and then. Glad to hear they're coming out of theirs."

Kenzie smiled as Alice Kate turned her attention to a newly arrived customer. But inside, she was trying to put the pieces of the puzzle together. She would have to ask her mother about that second mortgage. About everything, come to think of it. Kenzie hadn't told her parents the truth about Denver, and now she was finding out they hadn't exactly been truthful with her either. In a strange way, that made her feel better. She guessed the acorn didn't fall far from the tree after all.

The pizza smelled great, and back at the Feed and Grain, it tasted even better than it smelled. Kenzie ate two big slices and had to fetch paper towels from the restroom, because the little napkins from Itty Bitty weren't nearly enough to wipe the heavenly grease from her fingers.

She and Cody watched Taylor open the Coke dispenser and they each took a can before she locked it back up. "Employee perks," laughed Taylor. After Cody headed back to the loading deck, Taylor watched the cash register while Kenzie worked at stocking shelves.

At ten to four, Taylor took a hundred dollars out of the till and tucked it into Kenzie's back pocket.

"You don't have to do that," said Kenzie. "This is only my fifth day."

"And you haven't had a paycheck yet. This week's check will come next Friday. I saw your sandwich yesterday. I assume today's was similar. I like you, Kenzie. I hope you stay and run your parents' farm. Consider this a little gift. It sounds terrifying to be broke."

It was the most pleasant day Kenzie had had in a long time. Everything about it had been positive. She pushed worry to the back of her mind and chatted with Taylor, or rather listened to Taylor go on and on about her husband Axel and their reindeer.

When she had a chance, she said as casually as she could muster, "Say, you haven't heard anything else about that fellow who thought he found a wreck at the quarry, have you?"

Taylor shook her head. "Not about him, no. But Axel said one of the ranch hands from the Lazy B was thinking about sniffing around over there for car parts to salvage."

Kenzie's heart pounded against her breastbone, and she felt a sudden need to lean against the counter.

"Time flies," said Taylor. "It looks like your chauffeur is five minutes early this afternoon. Why don't you go on? Sunny will be here any minute." She grinned.

Kenzie grabbed her purse and headed for the door. Halfway there, she turned around and went back to give Taylor a hug. "Thanks for everything." Then she left.

♡

After Clayton dropped Kenzie off at work that morning, he'd headed back to his hotel room. It was getting smaller by the day, or so it felt, but he needed the protection of walls before calling his father. And he certainly didn't want to engage him in conversation while sitting behind the wheel of his borrowed Mercedes.

He had gotten so wrapped up in Kenzie and his growing fondness for her that he'd practically forgotten the reason for running away to Colorado. His father's voice brought it all back to him.

"You irresponsible pup! What am I going to do with you? Didn't Polly tell you I was calling?"

"Actually, Dad, she told everyone else many times over. Does that count?"

"Don't start with that smart mouth. I told you, what happened with Lulamae years ago is none of your business, and Polly agrees."

"Really? I had the distinct impression that if I bought her another chocolate milkshake, she would reveal every secret she possesses."

Plano made a rude noise. It took Clayton a moment to realize his father was stifling a laugh.

"Don't worry, Dad. I'm not going to pry information out of her. You said you wanted me to leave that all alone, so…are you sitting down? I'm not going to go there. If you don't want me to figure out what kind of hold Lulamae has on the family, then I'm not going to waste time on it."

Plano's tone turned suspicious. "What are you doing up there in Eagle Town?"

"Eagle's Toe," corrected Clayton. "Austin sends his love. Thor and Ashley are doing great, and frankly I don't know how they put up with Polly. She comes to visit for three months! She plans to stay until New Year's."

"She is besotted with her grandchildren."

"Is that what you call it?"

Plano made another strangled noise.

"Are you all right?"

"I'm trying not to laugh at my poor sister."

"Well, she's anything but poor. She was complaining at dinner that her caretakers at the Texas ranch want a raise. And she cannot understand why they refuse to take care of the dogs while she's gone."

"What happened to her kennel workers?"

Clayton stretched out on the bed and turned on the Weather Channel.

He punched mute. "She said they got a better offer. Her caretakers are nice enough, she says, but they're afraid of the Dobermans."

"She told me she was downsizing," grumbled Plano.

"She is. She brought the Chihuahuas with her, but Thor didn't want six more Dobermans in the house with the little ones. The kids, I mean."

"Are they cute?"

Clayton smiled at the thought of those angelic faces. Then he frowned. "Wait a minute. You haven't seen them?"

"Polly sent pictures. But kids are different in three-dimensions."

It was Clayton's turn to chuckle. "They are the cutest darned things I ever saw."

"Hmmm," said Plano. "That's something I never heard you say before." His tone grew suspicious again. "Are you thinking of hiring a girl to play your wife so you can trick me into letting you have your inheritance?"

Clayton's face fell. How did his father know he'd even considered such an option?

Plano laughed out loud. "I guessed right, didn't I? Your old man has been around the block a few times, you know."

"Well, for your information," said Clayton, gathering his wits, "I have no intention of doing any such thing. In fact, if I do get married, I won't even tell you about it. How's that?"

"What? Are you saying you actually met someone? Is this one of those sob-story waitresses you used to date?"

Clayton marveled at how different the world looked to him now. "I'm not telling you anything, Dad." He kept his tone civil. "No matter what I do, you will accuse me of trying to trick you into releasing my inheritance. So I guess the best thing would be to never tell you anything about her." He bit his tongue.

"So there is someone."

"It doesn't matter, Dad. It's not like I could invite you to a wedding now, is it? You wouldn't believe it was real."

"Well, that Mercedes you're driving is real, and it belongs to me."

"You don't sound too upset about it."

Plano hemmed and hawed. "I guess it's fine. I don't want you driving some POS rental car. What do you want me to do with this here Maserati parked in my garage?"

Clayton stood up and pulled a can of Coke loose from its plastic mooring. Then he sat down at the table and popped the top. "I'll tell you what, Dad. You were right about that car. It's too expensive for me, and it's not good for anything but showing off. Did those repo people leave you a card? Call them up and have them take it. I'm thinking of buying a tractor."

"What kind of fool stunt are you pulling? I asked Austin what you were up to, and he put that perky little wife of his on the phone. I thought she'd never hang up. Now you listen to me, Clayton. You are actually starting to make sense, giving up on the Lulamae thing and letting repo take the Maserati. But don't you go and marry any little spitfire babblefest like Erin. You hear? I'm going deaf in that ear, and I don't need another in-law talking in the other one. Now who is this girl you're seeing?"

Clayton sipped at his soda. "Dad, you only think I'm making sense because I actually agree with you about a couple of things. Crazy, huh? But you accused me of planning to trick you by getting married. Sorry. I can't let you anywhere near this woman. You'll mess things up for sure. So, even though you won't hear anything more until our first child is born, I still love you."

"Clayton! Don't you dare hang up that phone!"

"Just trying to save your hearing, Dad. Bye-bye." He ended the call and muted the phone. Sure enough, it began to vibrate like mad. He knew he would probably rue the day he'd hung up on his father, but Plano had thrown him for a loop. Not that Clayton wanted to involve Kenzie in a fake marriage. No way. And he couldn't stand the concept of pretending with someone else. The very thought disgusted him.

No. The idea of marrying Kenzie—now that his father had planted it in his mind—dazzled him. And think of how cute their kids would be!

"Good Lord, Clayton," he muttered to himself. "You've got it bad." He tossed the empty can in the trash and grabbed his keys. At least his dad wasn't too upset about him borrowing the Mercedes. And when Clayton told him to let the repo team take the sports car, be darned if he wasn't knocked back on his heels.

Clayton had seen a flower shop west of the elevators. He wondered if Kenzie liked roses. It was worth a shot. He'd told her he liked her a lot. Time to start showing it a bit.

He headed downstairs. In the elevator, he dialed the number he'd seen on the side of Brady Felton's tow truck. "Hello, Brady? This is Clayton Masters. You know, Jerk Face."

Brady laughed.

Clayton went on, "Say, I know this is a crazy question, but how much are tractors going for these days?…No kidding?…Do you mind if I drop by and ask you a few questions?… Thanks. See you soon."

Clayton ended up having lunch with Brady Felton. They actually did look at tractors, and Clayton was stunned at how much tractor he could get for one-fifth the price of his Maserati. They also checked out several other vehicles. Brady was a nice guy, and Clayton knew he had made a good impression when Brady took two hundred dollars out of his till and handed it over.

"What's this for?"

"That first day in the parking lot? I wasn't there looking for your Mercedes. I just took it so I could pretend to Kenzie that I was using your money to pay for repairs on her father's old truck."

"Keep it," said Clayton. "After all, I'll just be giving it back to you soon, if everything goes okay."

Sunny joined them for lunch. She brought hot soup and homemade sandwiches, and a checkered table cloth that she threw over the end of the counter. They ate standing up, but it was still a treat.

"This is delicious," said Clayton. "I can't tell you how much I appreciate it."

"Well, you're helping out the Shanes in a big way, so I'm glad to do it."

After their late lunch, he went to the Cattleman's florist, then headed for the Feed and Grain. He knew he was a wee bit early to pick up Kenzie, but he was looking forward to a nice reaction when she saw the red roses he'd picked out. They were in a green vase, supported by a box provided by the florist, but even so he'd driven five miles an hour from his parking space to the front of the Feed and Grain. He could see her inside at the cash register, gathering her things. A smile crept up from deep inside and threatened to strain his cheek muscles.

After talking to his father, he had realized that his feelings for Kenzie were real. He had fallen smack in love, and it couldn't have happened at a worse time. It totally ruined his oh-so-clever plan to arrange a marriage and fool his father. How could the old man know what he'd been thinking? That didn't matter now, because he would not allow Kenzie and his feelings for her to be tainted by deception, not even to gain a fortune.

Kenzie exited the store and moved so quickly he had no time to get out and hold her door. She slid into the car, her mind somewhere else.

"Bad day?" asked Clayton.

"Hmm? No, actually, it was a really nice one. At work." She sniffed the air. "Do I smell roses?"

Clayton was grinning from ear to ear. "I got you a little surprise." He reached behind the passenger seat and lifted the vase to the front.

Kenzie's eyes widened and her mouth formed a silent, "Oh!"

"Surprise!" said Clayton.

Kenzie's features softened. "These are beautiful," she murmured. "For me?"

Clayton nodded.

"Isn't this backward? I mean, you're the one doing me all the favors. I should be buying gifts for you."

"You're giving me an excuse to drive my father's best Mercedes. No other thanks are needed."

She gave him a mischievous look. "So, you did take your father's car, after all."

"Guilty as charged." Clayton wondered if he should risk yet another personal request. Well, if a dozen roses didn't soften the request, nothing would. So he cleared his throat. "Kenzie, I was wondering if you'd like my phone number so you can reach me if you need a ride for something other than work."

She looked pleased. Clayton silently congratulated himself.

Someone knocked on the glass of the Feed and Grain door. It was Taylor. She was motioning for Kenzie to come back inside.

Kenzie looked torn. She pulled her phone out of her purse. "Here, do you mind adding your info to my contacts? I need to run in and see what Taylor wants." She tossed her phone in Clayton's lap as she got out of the car.

Clayton fondled her phone. "I guess that's a yes," he mumbled. He opened her contacts list and added his name and cell phone info. Then he entered his street address. And his room number at the Cattleman's. Kenzie was still inside. He found her cell number and added it to his own phone. He was about to slip it back into her purse when it announced the arrival of a text message with what sounded like the horns of Sherwood Forest.

He knew he should ignore the text. After all, it was none of his business. Yet. How much leeway could he count on after a dozen roses and the consent to add his phone number to her contacts?

Curiosity got the better of him, and he thumbed the text open. It was from Todd, and all in caps.

"WHERE IS MY CAR YOU THIEVING WITCH? IF I DIE, MY BLOOD IS ON YOUR HANDS. DON'T MAKE ME COME FIND YOU. YOU KNOW WHAT I'LL DO."

Clayton's brow furrowed. When the car door opened, he nearly dropped the phone. Kenzie slid in and pulled the door shut, careful not to tip over the vase of roses.

She said, "I forgot to give her the key to the register." She glanced apologetically in his direction. When she saw the phone in his hand with the text on the screen, her features darkened. "What are you doing?" She grabbed the phone out of his hand.

Clayton was embarrassed. "I'm sorry. I added my contact info, and while I was doing that, this text came in." He kneaded the leather steering wheel cover. "Am I forgiven?"

Kenzie's mood seemed to change dramatically upon reading the text.

Clayton waited for her to say something, but when the silence stretched to several seconds he asked tentatively, "Is that the car you borrowed to get to Eagle's Toe?"

She nodded. She blanked the screen and dropped the phone in her purse. Then she put her head in her hands and made a sound like an angry cat.

Clayton gave her another few seconds, then prompted, "Should I be running for the hills?"

Kenzie sat up, her face drained of color. She sagged in her seat. "I really hate that guy," she said. "I tried not to ever admit that to myself, because my folks raised me not to hate anyone." She turned to face Clayton. "Will you do me a favor?"

"Of course."

"Can we take a detour on the way to my house? I need to check on something."

"I'm at your service," said Clayton, trying to inject a note of levity. "Do you need to see my White Knight license before we go?"

Kenzie sighed heavily, and Clayton thought her eyes might leak at any moment. She said, "Don't be so nice to me, Clayton Masters. You don't know what I've done."

Chapter Eleven

KENZIE SAID VERY LITTLE AS Clayton drove. She gave him a heads up about this turn or that turn until they took a right off the highway onto Old Quarry Road. She could feel it every time he glanced her way because his eyes were shooting questions at her. As he coaxed the Mercedes off the blacktop and onto the gravel, she decided he deserved some kind of explanation.

"All those texts from Todd...." She paused. "He keeps threatening me about his car, but I don't understand why the police haven't knocked on my door yet. I mean, wouldn't you report someone for stealing your car if you were mad enough to make all those threats?"

"Does he know where your parents live?"

"He has a vague idea. I'm sure I mentioned Eagle's Toe a couple of times during the past year. But he doesn't have their street address. I never felt comfortable discussing my family with him."

"You had good instincts," said Clayton. "But if you don't mind me saying so, anyone who threatens to kill himself over a missing car...well, that can mean only one thing."

"And what might that be?" asked Kenzie. "That he's a nut case? I finally figured that part out on my own."

Clayton shook his head. "Not just that. It suggests to me that it's about more than the car."

Kenzie's brow furrowed. "Like what?"

"Let's find out."

Dark clouds were rolling in, heavy with rain, and the air smelled of ozone and the promise of a thunderstorm. She might be doing her chores

74

in the rain tonight. She chewed on a thumbnail until Clayton stopped the car. They were a good fifty feet from the edge of the quarry. He was obviously not taking his father's car anywhere near the brink.

Kenzie opened her car door. "We have to go right up to the edge," she said.

Clayton followed her silently, an arm's length away.

Kenzie wondered if he was worried she might shove him over, or maybe he was preparing to grab her if she tried to jump. For half a second, that thought seemed like a good idea. She could end it all and wouldn't have to face anything else.

But she dismissed it immediately. Her parents needed her, and if Todd was so desperate that he was texting about blood on her hands if he didn't get his Mustang back, he just might be in bigger trouble than she was, and no way did she want to miss that.

She stepped carefully as she neared the edge, very aware that Clayton had held back a few feet. The slope wasn't exactly ninety degrees, but it was steep enough that nothing had slowed the car on its way down except that one ledge that had tipped it upside down. She planted her feet firmly and craned her neck to peer into the shadows at the bottom of the quarry.

Yep, it was still there. No night watchman had discovered this particular wreck, and no sheriff had marked it off with yellow tape. She relaxed a bit and returned to Clayton. "Here's what it looked like after I shoved it over," she said, pulling her phone out of her pocket and showing him the picture of the wreck. "This one is how it looked before."

"Wow," said Clayton. "Remind me not to loan you the Mercedes."

Kenzie snorted. "Don't worry. I only trash the cars of men I hate." Her words were vindictive, but her tone was sad. "I was planning to send him a picture of the wreck, but I chickened out. And then he started sending me all those texts. He does sound pretty desperate, doesn't he?"

Clayton nodded. He took her hand. "Do you mind? I really hate heights." He inched toward the edge.

"I'll be your counterweight," she said.

Clayton leaned to study the wreckage. After five seconds, he had to pull back. "I don't see anything down there other than the car. Come on," he said, tugging her gently toward the Mercedes. "This gravel road runs around the lip of the quarry. Let's follow it a ways and see if there's a way down."

Kenzie let him lead her to the car and open her door for her. "What do you think we'll find?" she asked.

"I have no idea. Scratch that. I do have an idea, but there's no sense speculating until we take a look." He got behind the wheel and flicked the headlights on. The clouds made it darker than usual for four-thirty.

"Don't get too close to the edge," said Kenzie.

"My thought exactly," he replied.

They drove slowly for nearly a mile, seeing nothing but gravel and grasses and the two barely visible ruts that made up the little road. At last, Clayton said, "That's what I was hoping to find."

Kenzie saw that the road veered off to the side and seemed to drop into the quarry. A metal gate blocked the entry. A coil of heavy chain fastened one end of it to a wooden post. It looked like there might once have been a line of posts stretching away from the gate in either direction, but all that was left was some strands of barbed wire that leaned into the gap. She frowned.

"That road doesn't look wide enough for the Mercedes," she said. "I know there's a main gate somewhere across from the spot I pushed the car over."

"Why didn't you use it?" asked Clayton.

"Duh," she teased. "Because it's padlocked shut and sits even with the bottom of the pit. No cliff to shove the car over. But then again, I don't want us to end up at the bottom of the quarry like the Mustang. Your father would call the cops for sure."

Clayton flashed a grin. "When did you meet my old man?" he teased. He nodded toward the gate. "If we move that chain and post, it will be obvious that someone went down there looking for something. There's a flashlight in the glove box. Grab that, and let's see if we can navigate this wagon trail to the bottom on foot."

Kenzie fetched the flashlight. "This is really decent of you," she said. "You're going way beyond the dozen-roses mark. I'm going to owe you big time for this."

Clayton smiled. "That was my plan all along," he joked. "Nothing brings a man and woman closer faster than trespassing."

Kenzie laughed, a high-pitched sound.

Clayton took her hand. "Don't worry," he said. "The way this town talks about your family, you could probably come in here with a bulldozer and no one would say a word."

Kenzie followed as he slipped under the metal bar of the gate. She liked the feel of her hand in his. It reminded her of a summer by the river when she was thirteen. On the other side was a boys' camp, or maybe there were girls there, too. She couldn't remember any faces but one, that of a shy athletic boy who stood on a rock at the river's edge and peered at her through binoculars. She'd come every afternoon at the same time and looked back at him. On the fourth day, she'd borrowed her father's binoculars, the ones he used for deer hunting, and when she reached the usual spot, she lifted them to her eyes and was startled at how close he seemed. It was as if she could reach out and touch him. Then he lowered his, giving her a chance to see his face. She remembered every freckle. His cheeks were still hairless, but there was promise in his jawline. The sight of him took her breath away and made her heart pound.

That was what she was feeling now with her hand clasping Clayton's. A very pleasant tingle of electricity flowed up her arm and into various parts of her anatomy. She pretended the exercise was to blame.

The road deteriorated quickly from two ruts to one. The switchbacks made it clear that this part of the trail had never been intended for four-wheeled vehicles. By the time they reached the bottom, Kenzie was forced to hang back and follow in Clayton's footsteps, but he never let go of her hand.

♡

Clayton hoped he was doing the right thing. Had he fallen in love with a crazy woman? How much strength and resolve had it taken her to shove that car over a cliff? In contrast, he didn't even want to confront his own father about matters as simple as the details of his mother's trust. Maybe he should be more like Kenzie.

And what if they found a body in the trunk of that car? Was he going to continue to trust and admire her?

Yes.

The answer came so fast, his head spun. Not a good thing on a path that had narrowed to one lane, like a downhill trail at the Grand Canyon. His fear of heights was genuine, and he hadn't expected this hike to require clinging to the wall of the quarry. But he had her hand in his, and it was worth risking life and limb for that accomplishment.

Even so, he was relieved when they reached the bottom of the quarry. He looked around to orient himself. He'd thought he could look across the flat bottom and spot the red Mustang, but there were a surprising number of hefty slag piles dotted about. They weren't that noticeable from up on the edge, but they were tall enough that they obstructed the view at ground level.

He pointed across the quarry. "What do you think? That direction?"

Kenzie stood silently, gazing up at the trail they had just come down. Then she let her eye follow the rim. It stood out dark against the paler wall. After a few seconds, she pointed a few degrees to the right of

Clayton's angle. As explanation, she offered, "I figure the Mercedes is—" She zigzagged a finger back up the trail. "—right about there. We drove a mile, more or less, and that would put our starting point right about there. Drop a line, head for it."

Clayton was impressed. "No kidding? I always suspected women were smarter than me. I just expected they would be kind enough to hide that fact."

Kenzie laughed softly.

The unexpected sound was music to Clayton's ears. He grinned.

Kenzie confessed. "Also, when I was up there last Saturday, I was staring into the setting sun, so I was on the east side of the quarry. I'm just pointing to a spot opposite where the setting sun would be, if it weren't behind the clouds. Don't worry. I grew up here. I know the area. Let's go before we lose the rest of the light."

Clayton aimed the flashlight in the direction she pointed. "After you?"

Kenzie smiled shyly. She wiggled her fingers inside his hand. "I sort of like walking side by side."

Clayton puffed up a bit and struck off toward the point where he hoped they would find the car. It didn't take nearly as long as navigating the switchback to the bottom.

Kenzie clutched his hand. "There it is."

Clayton's brows rose. "You pushed that over the cliff?"

"It was in neutral."

Clayton murmured, "Wow. Remind me not to lend you the Mercedes."

Kenzie gave him a friendly shove. "The Mercedes is safe. You haven't ruined my life or stolen from me to pay for car parts." She walked around the wreck.

"It's a mess," said Clayton. "I take it, this used to belong to Todd?"

"Still does, if you're talking registration. I used it to drive home, then realized it was the only thing he really loved, and I was overcome with a burning desire for revenge." She spoke evenly, as if reading off a menu. Like someone who had grown numb inside.

"Well, this could easily be why he's screaming at you on the phone about his car." Clayton cringed inwardly at the crushed front end and the flattened roof.

"No," said Kenzie. "It has to be more than that. He's telling me his life is in danger. No one cares about the car but him, as far as I know. So why should anyone threaten him over the Mustang?"

"Then maybe it's something else. Something inside the car. You checked the trunk?"

"I opened the trunk to retrieve my suitcase, but I wouldn't classify that as checking it."

"Nice distinction," said Clayton with a smile. He noted that one of the car's hubcaps had popped loose on impact and lay a few feet away. "Is there a crow bar in there? Maybe he hid something in the hub caps."

"Be careful," said Kenzie. "It doesn't look all that stable."

Clayton's pulse sped up a bit when he realized that she was worried about him getting hurt. He squared his shoulders. "I'll see if I can open the trunk." The car had landed on its roof, and most of the other damage had been done to the front end which had collided with the outcrop of rock on the way down. He handed her the flashlight. "Hold it steady for me. I'm going to pop the trunk." He expected resistance but the trunk lid opened easily and thumped against the ground. Nothing. He squatted down to take a closer look and was pleased when Kenzie joined him, aiming the flashlight at the interior. One corner of a carpet square had jostled loose.

"What is that for?" asked Kenzie.

"It covers the tire well for the spare. Something must be holding the tire in place. Usually there are some tools stored with it. Here. I'll show you." He reached for the edge of the carpet and yanked it free. There was no tire or tools, but the space was jam-packed with something.

Clayton frowned at it. "What the heck?" He reached in and grabbed a handful and jerked it loose. When the first one dislodged, the entire contents of the tire well emptied onto the ground.

Kenzie shone the flashlight on it. "Oh my God," she whispered. "No wonder he's having a fit."

Chapter Twelve

"BUNDLES OF MONEY!" KENZIE picked up two from the pile that had fallen from the trunk. She felt like her eyes might pop out of her head. She aimed the flashlight at the rubber-banded bills in her hand. "These are hundreds." Her voice dropped to a low murmur. "Hundreds of hundreds. That means thousands. That rat was hiding money in his car, but still took out credit cards in my name."

Clayton peered about. "It's getting pretty dark. How long does twilight last here? I can see some stars in the east." He touched her hand. "Does that watchman work every night?"

Kenzie understood what he was saying right away. She turned off the flashlight, and they gave their eyes a chance to adjust. While they waited, she tucked the stack of bills she was holding inside her shirt. After a few moments, Clayton spoke in a hushed tone.

"If that watchman finds this car…" He left it hanging. "We need to hide this money until we figure out what's going on. We can't carry all this back to the Mercedes, especially since we'll need to use the flashlight to make our way up that switchback."

As Kenzie's eyes adjusted, she could see his worried expression. "Do you think it's illegal? I mean, maybe it's drug money or something."

"I thought weed was legal in Colorado."

"Don't be silly. I mean like heroin. I never saw Todd use it, but I'll bet his motorcycle buddies did all kinds of stuff."

"That might explain why he's worried about his welfare. Although, it would make more sense if these bundles were drugs. If he were selling for someone, he could be in big trouble for losing the goods."

"Maybe he'd made the sale and hid the money. Maybe he hadn't had a chance to move it yet." Kenzie cupped her hand around the bundle under her shirt. She chewed her bottom lip. "I don't think he was robbing banks or anything."

"Would he have told you if he was?"

"No. He called me 'eye candy' and 'booty call' when his friends were around. I guess he never really returned my feelings. I mean, my original attraction to him. That bad boy thing they talk about? It must be real. I had it really bad for a while. But when the haze began to clear, I realized he was using me. I don't think he would have told me anything like that. Who knows? Maybe he's one of America's most wanted bank robbers."

Clayton said, "Let's hide this stuff. There's a slag pile between us and the main entrance. We can scoop out a hole and shove these bundles in it. At least until we figure out what to do about all this."

Kenzie's heart leapt. "Can I keep it? Lord knows, he swindled me out of thousands and ruined my credit. The only thing worse than his texts are the calls from collection agencies that I keep ignoring."

Clayton was already moving bundles of money. "Let's get it hidden. If it's from a robbery, he might claim you're an accessory or something."

Kenzie followed him to the slag pile, her arms full of money. Her bitterness was evident in her voice. "Don't tell me. That jerk has messed with me again. How much trouble am I in this time?"

Clayton began scooping out rocks and dirt from the side of the slag pile that loomed above them in the dark. Kenzie went back to the car for more bundles. When they had transported the last of the money to the slag pile, Clayton began shoving it into the hole. Then he pushed the stones and dirt back up the side of the pile, covering the money. "Let's not forget where we hid it."

"Oh, that would be just perfect, wouldn't it?"

"Nice sarcasm," teased Clayton.

"It's one of the many services I provide," Kenzie muttered. She froze as Clayton's arm slipped around her shoulders.

"It's getting cold," he said. "I think we should get out of here and figure out what to do next."

"I have to get home and feed the animals."

"I'll help you. And then, if you'll let me, I'll take you out to dinner."

Kenzie was cautious. He was so darned nice, and she still had to suck in air when he smiled at her. His sensitive mouth and his boyish expressions warmed her heart...and other things, too. But could she trust him?

As if sensing her concern, Clayton added, "We need to talk about the ramifications of what we've found. Do you have a lawyer?"

"Do I need one?"

"Let's figure that out over dinner. Come on." He took her hand and tugged her gently away from the slag heap.

Kenzie tugged back. "You don't have a great sense of direction, do you? The trail is this way."

"See? We need each other."

Kenzie could hear the smile in his voice. She couldn't help but smile back, even though he probably couldn't see her face. "Wait! If we use the flashlight to light the path, anyone at the front gate might see us."

"Was there anyone in sight when you shoved the car over? Did anyone come running when it hit bottom?"

"No. I mean, I didn't stay around very long, but I think I would have noticed, right?"

"So we'll use our flashlight. If anyone sees us, we'll just say...we'll say we wanted to look at the stars." He squeezed her hand.

That gesture sent a shiver of pleasure through Kenzie. "All right," she said. She would have cupped both her hands around his, but one was cradling a bundle of cash inside her shirt. Then, "Have you ever done farm chores?"

"No. Why?"

"This should be fun." She grinned in the chilly night air.

♡

Clayton stuck to the inside of the trail and did not relax until it widened into a dirt road as they approached the rim. He still had Kenzie's hand firmly in his when he opened the passenger door of the Mercedes for her. She got in and turned off the flashlight.

Clayton got behind the wheel and started the car. The interior lights came on for a moment, and he found Kenzie watching him. The look in her eyes made him feel like a white knight saving a damsel in distress. Of course, he figured if he told her what he was feeling, she would punch him. They both looked away at the same moment. Then he turned the car around carefully and drove slowly back to the gravel road. The dashboard lights cast an eerie glow over the interior of the car. They hardly said a word all the way to her house. It looked uninviting. No lights were visible from the car.

Once there, she said, "I have to run upstairs for a moment. Check on my folks. Let them know I'm finally home."

"Okay. Want me to wait out here?"

"No, silly. You bought me flowers. I'll introduce you."

Clayton laughed softly. "It's good to have a pay scale. Let me carry those in for you."

"Thanks."

Clayton was out and around the car in a flash, although she'd already exited.

"Oh," she said. "That was very sweet." She just wasn't used to being treated nicely. "Thank you."

"I didn't do anything." He shrugged, taking the roses.

"You were thinking about it, though. Come on. Watch your step. Mom forgot to turn on the porch light. She's been so preoccupied lately. Dad still isn't feeling well."

From inside came the barking of the dogs. "Well, they know someone is here." The first thing she did when she opened the front door was reach in and turn on the porch light. Two overweight Australian shepherds greeted them. "This is Caleb. That's Cotton. They're pretty much retired now that we don't have sheep." She shook her head sadly. So much had changed since she went away to college. Her parents had barely mentioned any drastic changes. Or had they? Had she just been too wrapped up in her own life to notice?

She swallowed a dose of guilt. She tended to rush through their letters because they were always bragging about one of her siblings. Promotions, deployments, foreign ports of call. Did she miss the important parental changes because she resented all the attention her siblings got?

She flipped a second switch, and two lamps glowed softly in the living room. She led Clayton into the room. "They must be upstairs. Mom? I'm home. Sorry I'm late."

Right on cue, there was a shuffling sound from upstairs.

"Wait here, Clayton. I'll be right back." She took the stairs two at a time. Her parents' bedroom was at the back of the house, at the opposite end from her own. She saw the door open as she approached. Her mother's hair looked unkempt.

"Mom? Is everything okay?"

"Hi, Kenzie." Marigold kept her voice down. "Your father is still resting. I lay down beside him for a few minutes and must have fallen asleep." She patted her hair. "I can make soup for dinner."

"No worries. Clayton is downstairs. He's going to help me with the chores, and then he invited me to dinner in town." Kenzie peered past her mother. All she could see was her father's bare feet on the foot of the bed. "His feet look cold. Maybe he needs a blanket."

"I'll take care of that. Is this the same Clayton who's been driving you to and from work?"

"Yes." Maybe now was not the time to introduce them. "You relax, okay? I'll make sure you're properly introduced in the morning. How's that?"

Marigold nodded. She looked distracted.

"Dad still refuses to call the doctor?"

"Oh, honey, you don't call them out anymore. You have to drive into town with an appointment."

"Clayton could take you."

"Nobody has office hours now."

"How about the hospital?"

Marigold shushed her. "Don't say that word. I tried at lunch, and he got so upset. He claims he'll be fine. He said he can't even catch a bug around here without me nagging at him." Her eyes glistened. "You got a pain?" She glanced at the hand Kenzie was still pressing against her shirt.

"No, I'm fine." Kenzie frowned. "Are *you* all right?"

"Just worn down, honey." She lowered her voice to a murmur. "Men are lousy patients."

Kenzie smiled. "I'll remember that," she said. "If you hear a commotion out back, Clayton is going to help with chores, and the pigs haven't met him yet. I shouldn't be too late."

Marigold nodded. She looked a tad more alert, so Kenzie planted a soft kiss on her forehead and waited until her mother closed her door before stepping quietly into her own bedroom. She opened the top dresser drawer and deposited the thick bundle of bills there. She took a moment to cover them with her clean underwear, then stifled a giggle. *Miss Rich Britches.* She shut the drawer and headed back downstairs.

She found Clayton examining the school pictures and family portraits hanging on the wall.

"Your siblings?" he asked.

"Yep. All three of them went into the service right after high school. I went to college. Lot of good it did me."

Clayton looked confused.

Kenzie said, "Never mind. Come on. You can shove your feet into my dad's barnyard boots so you don't ruin your shoes." She led the way through the kitchen, turning on lights as she went, and stopped in the mudroom to change into her muck-encrusted rubbers.

"I don't remember it raining recently."

Kenzie looked at him in disbelief and laughed. "You never know what you're going to step in," she teased. "We'll feed the pigs first, because they'll make a racket if we don't."

Forty-five minutes later, Kenzie was still giggling as they arrived at the Cattleman's parking lot. "The look on your face when Emma demanded her Fig Newton!"

Clayton was smiling. "I swear, I never knew bacon came from an animal with so much personality. I don't think I can ever eat pork again."

"Giving it up is the least you can do," said Kenzie, "after you said to her face that she was the ugliest thing you'd ever seen. That was harsh."

"How was I supposed to know she'd understand me?"

"Pigs are smart," said Kenzie.

"And huge."

"How come you know nothing about animals? Axel Garrison runs an animal sanctuary, and your aunt Polly has a huge ranch in Texas."

"My father has an estate in east Texas, but the closest thing he has to a barn is an eight-car garage. And then, when I was about ten, I was shipped off back east to an expensive boarding school."

Kenzie made a mental note to delve into that later. She could tell from the change in his voice that it bothered him a lot. Her smile faded. "My folks used to have twenty-two sows and a couple of boars. They sold baby pigs every year. They used to keep a hundred goats. Now they have ten. And when I left for college, they had three hundred head of cattle. Now they have six."

Clayton killed the engine. "You're really worried about them, aren't you?"

Kenzie nodded. She took a deep breath. "Dad claims he has a bug. He wants us to quit talking about doctors and hospitals."

Clayton took her hand. "My dad is the same way. He got sick a couple of years ago and claimed he'd be fine in the morning."

"Was he?"

"Sure. They took out his appendix at two a.m., and by eight, he was feeling much better."

Kenzie made a disgusted noise. "You're supposed to be cheering me up! Besides, my dad had his appendix out in his twenties." She chewed her thumbnail.

"Il Vaccaro?"

"Hmm?"

"For dinner," said Clayton.

"We have stuff to talk about," said Kenzie. "Let's do the Itty Bitty. It's quieter."

She was pleased by Alice Kate's effusive greeting. "There you are! Twice in one day. How do I rate?" She opened her chubby arms and embraced Kenzie.

"Hi, Mrs. McAvoy. It looks like I'll be sticking around, so you'll probably get tired of me before long." When the hug ended, she dropped her head shyly. "This is my friend, Clayton."

"Clayton Masters." He smiled and extended a hand.

Alice Kate shook it warmly. "Austin and Erin were here for dinner last night. They told me his brother was in town. You're a might taller than Austin."

Clayton chuckled. "I love that little guy, but yeah, we're a little different."

"Are you taking Kenzie to the party Sunday?"

Kenzie looked a question at Clayton. "What party?"

"I was just about to ask the same thing," he said.

"Sorry," said Alice Kate. "I hope it wasn't a surprise. Austin said Thor and Ashley are having a barbecue for you on Sunday, but if it keeps getting colder, they'll do dinner indoors instead."

"Thanks," said Clayton. He slipped an arm around Kenzie. "Shall we make it a date?"

Kenzie was pleased, but she wondered if she'd be able to leave her parents for that long. "I'd love to," she said. Then she added, "Let's see how my dad is feeling."

They took a corner table, the one farthest from the door. Alice Kate brought them a menu.

"Two choices tonight. Prime rib or roasted salmon."

Kenzie ordered the salmon and Clayton ordered the prime rib. When Alice Kate left, he leaned toward Kenzie and said softly, "I'm glad the cattle don't have as much personality as the pigs do."

Kenzie grinned.

They let the waitress bring coffee and water. Once she left, Kenzie leaned her elbows on the table. "Okay, let's get down to it. Am I going to need a lawyer?"

Chapter Thirteen

CLAYTON LOOKED INTO Kenzie's dark brown eyes and felt himself falling into them. The intensity with which she repeated her question brought him back to the surface.

"Do I or don't I?"

"Hmm?"

"Need a lawyer?"

He reached for her hand and was pleased when she let him caress her slender fingers. He wanted to make everything okay, he wanted to fix it all. He wanted to erase everything about that lousy Todd from her mind. But how? He sipped at his water.

"I think getting a lawyer is a great idea. My father has tons on the payroll. Hmmm. On second thought, I'm not sure we need that kind of muscle yet. Besides, they're mostly corporate attorneys, and it sounds like Todd is dragging you into a more mundane mess. Is there a law office in Eagle's Toe?"

"I left for college at eighteen and the last thing on my mind was legal services, so I have no idea."

"Shall I Google it?"

Kenzie tweaked his hand gently. "Small town, remember?" She held up a finger and caught Alice Kate's attention.

"What can I do for you, sweetheart?" Alice Kate's gaze moved back and forth between them, including them both.

When Kenzie hesitated, Clayton spoke up. "Mrs. McAvoy, if a person needed a lawyer in this town, where would he go?" He phrased the question carefully to keep Kenzie's name out of it.

Someone at a different table piped up, "Pueblo." The other twenty customers laughed.

Clayton realized he'd better be careful about what he said here. Kenzie wanted a quiet place to talk, but now they had such a quiet place that everyone in the room could probably hear them. He looked up hopefully at Alice Kate.

She wiped her hands on her apron. "Ignore them. There's a nice young man, only been here a couple of years, getting his own practice started. He married a local girl, Jasmine. In fact, she used to waitress for me. Now she runs his office."

Kenzie perked up. "Jasmine Angel? I went to school with her."

"Well, it's Hutch now. Jasmine's brother and his family moved back here from Pueblo, so she didn't want to leave, and Ryan Hutch was tired of dancing to the tune of a big firm, so he opened his office here. I'll write down his number. You'll know him when you see him. He has dark blond hair, he's six foot three with blue eyes, and he still dresses like a city boy. But I guess he wants to look the part." She scribbled on a napkin and added his office address. "He's just on the south side of this block."

"Thanks," said Clayton. "I appreciate it."

When dinner came, they kept conversation to a minimum but managed to smile a lot.

Clayton loved the way Kenzie would peek at him, then look away shyly. He decided the prime rib was the best he'd ever eaten. He even ate the asparagus. Everything tasted better when he was with Kenzie.

He felt his phone buzzing in his pocket. He ignored it. But by the third time, Kenzie leaned forward and murmured, "You can take that if you have to."

Clayton gave her an apologetic grimace as he pulled out his phone. He glanced at it. "It's my father," he said. "Let me just text him that I'll call him later."

Kenzie looked wistful. "My dad wouldn't know what to do with a cell phone. I'm glad yours is a bit more in touch with the modern world."

Clayton put the phone away. "I guess it's a good thing. Of course, your dad isn't interrupting our meal." He winked at her.

Alice Kate arrived as their plates emptied. "Dessert is on the house," she said. "And it's coming right up. Crème brulée." She stacked their empty dishes and, before she left, said, "Kenzie, did you have a chance to ask your mom if she's going to continue growing organic vegetables and strawberries for my kitchen?"

"Not yet, but I will."

"Excellent. Whenever you get a chance. I'll pack up what the cook collected for your pigs." She smiled and left.

Kenzie frowned.

"Problem?" asked Clayton.

"Oh, it's just that I don't remember my mother saying anything about going organic in her letters. How could I have lost track of them like that?" She added sadly, "They look so old."

Clayton gave a little shrug. "Our parents age, but we're too busy growing up to realize it, until one day…boom…they look like our grandparents."

"Exactly," said Kenzie.

"Did you keep her letters?"

Kenzie's eyes widened. "Yes! I have them all, zipped inside my suitcase."

"Maybe later you can go through them again, see what you missed."

"Have your parents turned into old people, too?"

The question brought Clayton up short. "Well, my dad looks the same to me, but his hair is starting to turn salt-and-pepper. Maybe he looks the same because he sounds the same. You know, when he's giving me a hard time."

Kenzie giggled. "I can't imagine anyone giving you a hard time."

"He thinks I should be more serious. He thinks I'm a playboy, running around in a fast car and doing nothing with my life."

Kenzie's eyes darkened with feeling. "I don't get that vibe from you at all." She suddenly looked uncertain. "Is that what we're doing? Am I just a notch on a playboy's pistol? Is that what you're after?"

"No!" He took both her hands in his. "Nothing could be further from the truth. Honest." He glanced about self-consciously and lowered his voice. "From the moment I first laid eyes on you, I was completely in your power. You're the most beautiful woman I've ever met. I'm just drawn to you."

"Like a moth to a flame?" she teased.

Clayton smiled. "I don't have any burns yet." He paused while dessert and coffee were delivered. Then, "It's almost ten. Don't they close soon?"

"Mrs. McAvoy will let us finish dessert. She just locks the door at ten. Puts out the 'Closed' sign." She whispered, "Her waitstaff probably has to be home before eleven on a school night."

Clayton chuckled. "Well, it's Friday, so I guess we'll have time to finish."

Kenzie tasted her dessert. "This is great." She moved her head in a way that included everything about the evening.

"Thanks," said Clayton.

"So, what about your mother?"

Clayton fussed with his napkin. "She's gone."

"Oh, I'm so sorry. You already told me that, didn't you?" She took another bite and diplomatically changed the subject. "Ten o'clock seems so early to go home. If you like, I'll give you an after hours tour of the highlights. You have to see my high school. I was a soccer star my senior year."

"No kidding? I'd love that. I played lacrosse."

Kenzie looked puzzled. "I've never seen that sport out here."

"It's an east coast thing. And…" he hesitated.

She finished for him. "And you are related to the Garrisons so your family has money and you went to a private school."

Clayton was surprised. "What exactly did you major in? Criminal justice? All these deductions."

Kenzie put a spoonful of dessert in her mouth and rolled it around in a way that made Clayton tingle all over. Then she smiled and said, "The Mercedes was a clue. And also I asked Taylor about you. Is Axel your cousin, too?"

"He's my cousins' cousin, but when we were kids, none of that mattered. We thought of ourselves as one big bunch of kids who were somehow related. And that was good enough." He scraped the bottom of his dish and waggled his eyebrows. "What else did Taylor tell you?"

Kenzie laughed softly. "Enough to make me feel okay about you driving me to and from work."

♡

They were the last ones out the door. Kenzie loved the way Clayton held her hand. In all the confusion going on in her life, there was one thing she knew for certain. This man was very important to her. She was filled with a need to get everything else behind her so she could concentrate on Clayton.

He held her car door, and after he slid behind the wheel, Kenzie said, "I don't want this evening to end."

"Me neither."

Kenzie allowed herself to be pulled into a tender kiss. It was brief, but the chemistry knocked her back, breathless. She cleared her throat. "If you go out the western side of the parking lot, I'll direct you to my high school. You've seen the farm. Other than that, the high school is where I spent the most time. Unless…."

"I would love to see your high school," said Clayton. "By the way, what time does the coach turn into a pumpkin?"

Kenzie sighed. "I said I wouldn't be too late. Maybe midnight?" She shook her head and laughed. "I feel like a high school kid all over again. Worrying about curfew."

Clayton leaned in for another brushing of lips. "Midnight it is." He added in his most exaggeratedly sexy voice, "Now where is this magical high school you speak of?"

Kenzie laughed out loud. "You better crack the whip over the white horses," she said, "if we want to squeeze in the whole coach tour before midnight."

The dark, empty school seemed lonely and sad to Kenzie. Without its students and faculty, it was just a big old building. "Pull around the back," she said. "There's a student parking lot way out by the playing field."

As soon as Clayton parked the car, she was out, striding toward the track that surrounded the field. The evening air was crisp and getting colder. She rubbed the goosebumps off her arms.

"This is it?" asked Clayton dramatically. "This is where a star was born?"

Kenzie smirked at him. "You are adorable, but you have an annoying smart mouth." She softened her comment by slipping an arm around his waist. "I'll have you know, I broke four different high school records in track."

"I thought you played soccer?"

"I did it all. I was the best athlete at the school."

Clayton humphed. "Probably the best female athlete."

Kenzie pulled away and pretended to be horrified. "I cannot believe you said that, Mr. Masters! I'm going to have to write a letter to the Department of Education and file a lawsuit. Something under Title IX, I think."

Clayton played along. "It's a good thing Mrs. McAvoy gave me the number of a good lawyer."

"Ha!!! I'm the native daughter here. I get the local guy. You'll have to use your father's lawyers."

"No worries. No court would rule against me anyway. I'm a man, after all." He puffed up his chest and struck a pose like Superman. "Everyone knows men are better athletes."

Kenzie shrieked in mock fury. "You will eat those words, Jerk Face. Think you're so athletic? I'll race you around the track. One, two, three, go!"

She said it so fast, she caught him off guard. Before he could react, she was off and running.

"Hey!" But Kenzie was laughing over her shoulder. Clayton started running.

Kenzie set a nice pace for herself. She'd kick it into gear if he got too close. She peeked over her shoulder and was gratified to see that he was chasing her. The whole thing sent a thrill through her that she'd never felt before. Gorgeous Clayton, chasing her through the night, all alone, no one else around. She let her mind wander for a moment down one of many possible paths this romantic pursuit might take. The sound of Clayton's footsteps pounding up behind her snapped her out of her reverie. She spared him a quick glance.

"Holy mackerel," she said. "You're fast!"

When he grinned back at her, clearly anticipating victory, she added, "For a boy!" And she kicked it into overdrive. She realized after a few seconds that she couldn't hear Clayton behind her. She kept going, back to their starting point. After all, it was only a quarter of a mile.

Barely breathing hard, she turned to locate him. He was loping slowly across the grassy edge of the field.

"Cheater!" she called out. "Come on, I'll give you another chance. I'll even it up a bit. I'll run backwards."

Now he was only a few feet away, but he was laughing so hard, he had slowed to a crawl. Gasping for breath, he said, "Let's change sports. How about wrestling?" He grabbed for her.

Kenzie danced out of his reach. "Come on, you can do it," she taunted playfully. She motioned him to follow her back across the track to the inner field. The grass was damp. "Show me how to play lacrosse."

This time, he got his arms around her. "Hold on, hold on," he gasped. "Let me breathe for a second."

Kenzie struggled, but it was only an act. She stopped with his arms still around her. "I guess I should have told you I tried out for the Olympic team."

He pulled her closer. "Oh, thank goodness! I thought I was getting old as fast as our parents."

"Hardly." Her breath caught. Their lips were only inches apart. A moment later they were kissing again. Kenzie reveled in the soft sweetness of it, and when Clayton tried to tease her lips apart, she realized she was way too close to letting herself go. She ended the kiss, hating herself for doing so. "I'm sorry. We should go. I told Mom I wouldn't be too late."

Clayton seemed as breathless as she was. He nodded and tugged her by the hand in the direction of the car.

Once inside, she bounced the back of her head against the headrest. "Darn it! We had things to talk about."

Clayton grinned. "First thing tomorrow morning, I'll call this lawyer. Do you work tomorrow?"

"Thanks for understanding. I'm off tomorrow. Sunny takes Saturdays."

"Maybe we can see this guy tomorrow, then. I'll see if I can set something up, and then I'll call to let you know." He started the car. "And it gives me a great excuse to see you again."

Once they were parked in front of her house, a good-night kiss seemed in order. After what felt like days in a dream state, Kenzie noticed the dash clock. "Oh my gosh, we've been necking like teenagers for thirty minutes. See you in the morning." She felt herself leaning toward him again, but stopped herself with a determined growl. Clayton laughed, and somehow that made it easier to slip out of the car.

Once in the house, she moved as quietly as she could. It was almost one a.m. No light clicked on under her parents' door, so she eased into her room. She knew she should get some sleep, but her whole body felt like an electric current was moving through it. She was consumed with thoughts of Clayton. She ran the evening back through her memory, savoring every second. "Oh! He said I should read Mom's letters. Good idea."

She settled cross-legged on her bed and splayed the envelopes out before her. A task she thought would take fifteen minutes took fifty-five. She was surprised when she plugged her phone into the charger and saw that it was two a.m.

She kept reading things she barely remembered. She had a recollection of her sister making lieutenant, but none at all about the second mortgage mentioned in the same letter. Why had her parents taken out a second? She'd thought the farm was clearly theirs. Maybe they needed a loan, but what had they used it for? The house still needed painting, and the number of livestock had continued to dwindle. It was yet another mystery.

In the letters she'd received after graduating, her mother had begun hinting about her coming back to Eagle's Toe. But she never said anything about her father's health.

At least reviewing the letters had calmed her down, and she was ready for sleep. She got into her pajamas and crawled into bed. Before she even turned off the lamp, she sat straight up and threw off her covers.

The money!

She almost tripped over her own feet in her haste to reach the dresser. Then she resettled, cross-legged, on the bed, but this time, she was counting out stacks of hundred-dollar bills. Ten hundreds to a stack. When she finished, she had ten stacks and a couple hundred left over.

She rummaged in the nightstand for an envelope. Ten thousand dollars made a nice thick stack. She had to wrap a rubber band around it. On the front, she wrote, "Mom, I got a downpayment on the money I'm owed. This should help a bit. Love, Kenzie."

She would place it somewhere her mother would find it once Kenzie had left with Clayton to see the lawyer.

♡

Clayton barely recognized himself in the reflective surface of the Cattleman's lobby doors. Who was that dreamy-eyed guy with the smile on his face? Was this what love looked like? Or was it infatuation? He couldn't have fallen for a more complex woman. She certainly had some baggage haunting her. Not to mention the ex who was threatening her.

His shoes squeaked on the lobby floor. The grass around the track had been wetter than he thought. He'd have to set them on the heating unit in his room.

Kenzie could certainly run like the wind. Or maybe it only seemed that way because when he ran, he got winded. He chuckled at his play on words. He pushed the elevator call button. What a great evening.

Then he remembered the stacks of money hidden in the slag heap. "Okay," he said to his reflection in the elevator mirror, "what an *interesting* evening."

It was midnight, too late to call the lawyer Mrs. McAvoy had suggested. That would have to wait until morning. Still, he needed to talk to someone. He needed reassurance that everything would work out. Maybe Thor wouldn't mind filling him in on what he had discovered so far.

Stretched out on his bed, cell phone on speaker, he called his cousin. "Thor? I hope I didn't call too late."

"No, it's fine. Ashley and the kids are in bed, Mom is tucked away in her little cottage, and Rocky is asleep at my feet. I'm looking at expense spreadsheets, so I'm actually grateful for the interruption."

Clayton made a face and an expression from his childhood emerged. "Boo devil."

"You got it. If I don't keep up with it, January is a living hell. What can I do for you?"

Clayton fiddled with the remote, clicking the TV on and off again. "I was wondering if you'd had time to find out anything new about Kenzie's ex-boyfriend. He's begun threatening her, sending foul-mouthed texts."

"Really? What's that about?"

Clayton sighed. "Okay, here's the deal. Remember that Mustang I told you that Kenzie's ex is looking for? I found out tonight that Kenzie…sort of…borrowed the guy's car to drive home to Eagle's Toe. And naturally he wants it back."

"Sounds like she should comply and be done with it."

"It's a little more complicated than that. I have a feeling this guy is real bad news."

"Strange that she didn't know that."

"Oh, she suspects the same thing now. But you know, in the movies the bad guys keep their women in the dark. Could be something like that. I doubt Todd would have confided in her if he was doing something illegal."

"Like what?"

Clayton hesitated. Then he said, "You might check to see if any Denver banks have been robbed lately."

Chapter Fourteen

SATURDAY MORNING, KENZIE didn't even ask if her father was up to chores. She just went down and did them. After her shower, she took her time in her room, thinking about where to put the bundle of money so her mother could find it. She didn't want to hand it to her in person. That would mean answering questions. She was hoping, by leaving the note on the envelope, that her mother would accept the gift and be grateful enough to forego the interrogation.

She thumbed through another text from Todd. Her heart was closed to him now. It was as if someone else had run home to Eagle's Toe and pushed his stupid car into the quarry. He was just a problem to be resolved. And Clayton was going to help her.

She spent a few dreamy moments fondling the porcelain cowgirl and her horse. Maybe someday, she could have the horse she'd longed for as a child. That is, if her folks weren't losing the ranch.

At some point, she would have to ask her mother about that mortgage and where the money went. But for now, she pocketed her phone, on vibrate, for when Clayton called. He said he would after he reached that lawyer. She posed her figurines on the bed stand. She could finally hear movement downstairs, so she tucked the bundle of money into her shoulder bag and headed for the kitchen.

The house felt gloomy, and it was starting to smell like a sick room. She shook that off and detoured to the front windows to open the drapes. That cheered it up a bit. But the cheer didn't last. Her dad wasn't at the kitchen table. Her mother looked stooped and worn this morning.

"Dad's still feeling poorly?" She set her bag on the floor and retrieved mugs from the dish drainer.

Marigold filled them with coffee. "He says he's doing better. He didn't bite my head off about anything this morning. But I ordered him to stay in bed one more day. You don't mind, do you?"

"What? You mean the chores? No, of course not."

"You off work today?"

"Yes." She stirred sugar in her coffee. "Clayton is going to pick me up and...." She let it hang in the air. Did she really want to tell her mother they were going to see a lawyer?

"And?" prompted Marigold.

Kenzie thought fast. "And help me figure out a way to get us some transportation."

Marigold seemed pleased. "That would be nice. Did you get paid yesterday?"

"No, but I got a little advance on my wages. I didn't realize I'd have to wait another week to get paid for this one."

"I should have warned you. That's pretty common."

"Waitressing lets you take home tips every night," said Kenzie.

"I am amazed that you made enough to get a loan on a house."

Kenzie froze. Then she shrugged. "Some patrons are really generous."

"Even so, most young people can't get a loan for something like that with less than a year of waitressing behind them." Her tone was conversational, so Kenzie relaxed. Mom was probably trying to think of something other than Dad's health to talk about.

"Just lucky, I guess," said Kenzie. Then she rushed on. "I think we should plan on adding livestock in the spring. And Mrs. McAvoy wants to know if you're going to continue with your organic gardening. She says there's a growing demand for organic." Since Marigold showed no sign of starting breakfast, Kenzie got up and retrieved half a loaf of homemade bread from the breadbox and began cutting generous slices. "I can help you get that garden going again. I did a whole class at school on organic gardening and such." She returned to the table with butter and a knife and spread some on her slice of bread.

Marigold cupped her mug with both hands. "That's nice of her. She paid me way more than they were worth."

"That's the trick, Mom. People pay more for clean, organic food. We'll talk about that later, okay?"

Marigold seemed to perk up. "All right. Yes. We can plan around what she needs most. Ask her for input when you're in town."

Kenzie smiled. Somehow, grasping at straws, she had landed on a topic that lightened her mother's mood. She ate her bread and butter and sipped her coffee. The sound of footsteps upstairs made her mother jump, and a moment later, she was alone. Her phone vibrated. She closed her eyes and prayed it was Clayton.

Her prayer was answered. He texted, "On my way. We see Hutch at 10."

It would take him about twenty minutes to get to her, so she enjoyed her coffee and wondered what all the bumping around was upstairs. The minutes ticked by and she tried to construct a scenario in her head. Mom was helping Dad get dressed? Or maybe he'd stumbled against the nightstand? One particularly loud bang sent her to the bottom of the stairs. "Mom? Are you okay?"

Marigold's voice drifted down. "I'm fine. I accidentally slammed a door."

Hmmm. That didn't sound like her mom. Slamming doors was more Kenzie's style, or it was when she was a teenager. Maybe she was more like her mother than she thought. "Okay," she called up. "Clayton is on his way. I'll be back in plenty of time for chores."

No answer. Kenzie took that as an okay, and she returned to the kitchen to fetch her bag. Before she headed out to the porch to wait for Clayton, she looked for a place to put the money. For some reason, she wanted her mother to find it, not her dad. Then it came to her. The one place her dad never really dug around in was the refrigerator. That was her mother's domain. She supposed if he started messing around in the fridge, Mom might think he was capable of making his own sandwiches. She suppressed a grin as she opened the refrigerator door.

The shelves were nearly empty. Marigold hadn't been doing much cooking that week. But Kenzie found a half gallon of orange juice and a leftover bowl of lima beans. She tucked the bundle of money with her note behind the orange juice, and made a mental note to stop at a grocery store before she returned from town.

♡

Clayton woke up at the first light of dawn, filled with anticipation. He was going to see Kenzie today, and the memory of the night before made his skin tingle as if he were hooked up to an electric current. He showered and dressed, wondering what his father would think of him getting up so early. He was the "playboy" and the "ne'er-do-well" in his father's mind. Such stereotypes made it impossible for him to explain to his dad what he was doing with his ten thousand a month.

He spent ten minutes trying to figure out the in-room coffee maker, then ordered breakfast sent up. He sat at the little table by the window and counted the cash he had left. Three thousand two hundred. He'd covered his hotel bill and spent money on meals and gas and porcelain figurines and roses from the Cattleman's florist. The corners of his mouth turned up. The figurines had come from Ashley Garrison's art gallery. He decided he would take Kenzie there today and let her pick out another one. Or anything else she wanted. And there was that other bit of business he had planned. But first, he had to call Ryan Hutch.

By the time he finished his breakfast, it was nine o'clock. He dialed the number and was greeted by a pleasant feminine voice.

"Ryan Hutch, Attorney at Law. Jasmine speaking. What can I do for you?"

"Hello. I'm hoping I can make an appointment for today. Name is Clayton Masters. I'm from out of town."

"Oh, you're Austin's brother, right?"

Clayton was taken aback. "Um, yes. How did you know?"

"Austin and Erin came to our wedding, and we went to theirs. And Austin runs all his business arrangements through Ryan. Is ten o'clock okay? We want to go to the movies this afternoon."

Clayton chuckled. "This really is a small town. Sure, ten o'clock is perfect." He made sure he knew where he was going, then hung up and texted Kenzie.

He skipped The Muffin Man. He would take her to lunch after talking to Hutch. He also felt a growing concern about the money they'd buried in the slag heap. He knew it was probably ill-gotten gains, but the idea of someone else finding it and removing it made him feel like they'd be robbing Kenzie. Could he chance asking the lawyer about that?

He muttered in disgust, "Of course, you dingbat. That's what lawyers are for." Then he made another call. "Morning, Thor!"

"Clayton? Isn't this a little early for you? I seem to remember you never getting up before noon on a weekend."

"Times change," said Clayton, adding silently, *I never had a gorgeous woman waiting for me back then.* "Any news on that bad boy, Todd?"

"Give me a little time, man. We just talked at midnight. I should know more tomorrow. I'll fill you in then."

"At the barbecue?"

"Sure. We'll pull a manly escape act for a few minutes. Besides, my mother will want to interrogate your friend Kenzie."

Knowing Polly, Clayton figured Thor had used the right word. "Okay. I'll try to be patient. See you then."

He hung up and focused on driving. Kenzie was waiting for him on her front porch. She looked amazing in faded jeans, black flats, and a red sweatshirt, layered over something pink. She didn't even wait for him to come to a full stop. She scampered down the stairs and opened the door, tossing her leather bag on the floor.

"Good morning." Her voice was sweet, and she had a lovely smile for him.

Clayton was momentarily struck dumb by the joy he felt in her presence. He drummed his fingers on the steering wheel.

"Anything wrong?" asked Kenzie.

He cleared his throat. "I was just wondering if our good-night kisses meant a good-morning kiss was in order."

She laughed softly, leaned toward him, and kissed him gently on the lips. Her voice was huskier when she repeated, "Good morning."

Clayton was on Cloud Nine. "It is now." He grinned and turned the car around.

Ryan Hutch's law office was on the south side of the same block where Thor Security was housed. The old brick façade with the shiny brass nameplate projected a sense of class and gravitas, both of which set Clayton's mind at ease.

The young woman behind the desk was dressed for business, and a thick, plush carpet made Clayton feel that not even the walls would hear his secrets.

"Good morning," she said. "You must be Clayton." She stood up and extended a hand. "I'm Jasmine. I'll let Mr. Hutch know you're here." She paused, and a flash of recognition lit up her face. "Kenzie? Is that you? I heard you were back in town. Oh my gosh, it's so good to see you!" She rushed forward and gave Kenzie a warm hug.

Clayton cocked his head to one side. "Old friends?"

"And classmates," said Kenzie, hugging Jasmine in return. "Sorry I haven't called, Jazz. I've had a lot on my mind. I hope we can get together after—well, after your husband cleans up this mess for me."

"I hope it's nothing serious," said Jasmine. She led the way to Ryan's office door and knocked softly. "Ryan? Clayton Masters is here. And this is Mackenzie Shane, the greatest athlete our high school ever produced."

Clayton saw a blush creep up on Kenzie as Ryan waved them inside. Mrs. McAvoy had described him to a T—dark blond hair, six foot three, blue eyes, and a superbly tailored suit. Clayton and Kenzie took the chairs he indicated. "May I offer you coffee or tea? Or Perrier?"

Clayton said, "Nothing for me, thanks."

Kenzie added, "I just finished breakfast. But thank you anyway."

Ryan leaned back in his padded leather chair and looked from one to the other. "Now that we've met, and I've offered hospitality, what can I do for you?"

Clayton and Kenzie exchanged glances, but neither one spoke. Clayton wanted to explain the entire situation, but he thought Kenzie should present the story in the way that made her most comfortable. However, after a few seconds, Clayton realized that the only way Kenzie would be comfortable was by not talking at all.

Ryan broke the silence. "Why don't you start by telling me which of you is my client?"

Kenzie reached into her pocket and pulled out the hundred dollar bill that Taylor had given her the day before. She laid it flat on Ryan's desk and said, "I'm the one who's in trouble, so I think you should take my hundred as a retainer. I'm the one who really needs you. Clayton has done nothing except try to help me."

Clayton pulled out a hundred of his own, laid it next to hers, and said, "I am in this as deep as it gets. I don't want Kenzie facing it alone. She's had a rough time and there may be some trouble ahead for her, but I'm not leaving her side."

He was delighted when Kenzie turned to him, smiling warmly.

Hutch pulled the bills to the middle of his desk and set a paperweight on them. "Well," he said, "that's a beginning. Now, what's going on?"

Kenzie began, "We found some money. And we want to know if it's okay to spend it."

Clayton's eyebrows shot up. He held up a finger. "Just a second," he said, "I think we should go back to the beginning, don't you?"

Kenzie dropped her gaze to her hands and began to fidget. "I didn't want to tell him all about my bad choices."

Clayton said, "We both agreed that you need a lawyer, and maybe I do, too. The whole point of having a lawyer is being able to talk about your bad choices and know that your lawyer won't tell anyone."

Kenzie said, "I know you're right, but I just feel so stupid."

Ryan interrupted. "Let's start with the money. Where did you find it?"

Kenzie replied, "At the bottom of the old quarry."

Clayton added, "In the trunk of a wrecked car."

Ryan frowned as he pulled a yellow legal pad out of his drawer and began to take notes. "Not that it matters to me," he said, "but what were you doing in the old quarry? Necking?"

Kenzie blushed and said, "We were looking for something."

Ryan asked, "The money?"

Clayton said, "Not exactly. We weren't sure what we would find. Kenzie felt she had to go look, and I went with her. I've been driving her back and forth from work since her father's old truck died." He took Kenzie's hand and added, "I wanted to go with her. I'm really fond of her. And when I found out that she might be in trouble, I swore to myself that I would help her find a way out of it."

Ryan nodded. "Noble and admirable." He tapped his pen against the notepad. He focused on Kenzie. "Clayton said you felt that you had to go look for something. What inspired you to do that?"

Kenzie flashed a look at Clayton, and he squeezed her hand. She nodded ever so slightly and responded to Ryan's question. "I have an ex-boyfriend. He was never the kind of boy you would bring home to meet your parents. I was in my senior year of college, and I just had no idea what to do after graduation. I met him at a party. A frat party. It was months before I realized he'd never belonged to the fraternity. He had just crashed the party. Black jacket, leather pants, great big motorcycle. Lots of thick, curly black hair. And he had a sneer. You know, the kind that says, 'I don't care what your parents think of me.' Exactly what I thought I wanted."

Clayton covered his mouth with his free hand to hide a grin.

Kenzie shot him an irritated glance, but then had to smile herself. "I know it sounds stupid and young and dumb and all those other things," she said. "But when I left Eagle's Toe, I sort of screamed at my parents that I would never be back. So if I did come back I would have to eat those words. At the time I met Todd — Todd Wilson — he seemed like a reasonable alternative to crawling back home. But I was wrong."

Ryan nodded again. "Don't worry, Kenzie. We've all made silly mistakes in our lives. So you had an ex-boyfriend who turned out to be different than you expected?"

Kenzie laughed weakly. "You might say that. He turned out to be an absolute disaster. He always seemed to have pocket money, but he never seemed to actually pay for much. Looking back, I think it was an act. After what we found in the quarry, he obviously had tons. I went to work as a waitress, and I told him that I wanted to buy a house someday. Until then, we would have to rent a place. A few days later, he told me he had found us a house. I was over the moon. At that point, I still totally trusted him. All our belongings fit into suitcases. We managed to get them on the bike with us, and the next thing you know he's parking behind an old house in the historic part of Denver. We had to go in the back door and he was telling me the whole time it was a fixer-upper. That eventually we would get it all fixed up, but the first few months might be a little rough."

Ryan stopped her. "Did he tell you he had bought the house?"

"No." She paused, trying to remember. "I don't think he ever said that right out loud. He just let me believe that he had a right to be there. He didn't show me any documentation. And when I asked to see some later, he got angry and threw a temper tantrum. So I stopped asking. Looking back, I guess about two months ago I finally realized that we were squatting in that house." She shook her head sadly. "Every now and then, we had to take all our things out and go stay somewhere else for a day or two. Usually we camped out. After a while, he would take us back, and we would install ourselves there again. When I wasn't working, I tried to fix the place up. The big giveaway for me was when I tried to put curtains in the front windows. He threw a fit and tore them down. Then he took a hammer and replaced the plywood covering the windows, all the time yelling at me that I was not allowed to touch anything in the house. It was like living in a dumpster. I managed to get one room looking good enough and clean enough to sleep in. But he wouldn't let me touch anything else."

Ryan looked up from his notepad. "Where does the money come in?"

Clayton was watching Kenzie as she spoke. Now she turned to him, pleading silently for help. He took up the narration as best he could. "Apparently Todd was having a love affair with a classic Mustang. He was refinishing it. Rebuilding it. And he needed a lot of money for parts and paint, all those things. Kenzie was waitressing so she didn't have a lot of cash. Todd...." He hesitated and looked at Kenzie for permission to continue. She gave a little nod and he went on.

"Todd filled out credit card applications in Kenzie's name. I guess no one gave him a second look because Mackenzie could be a guy's name as well."

Ryan asked, "How many cards?"

Kenzie whispered, "Three."

Clayton continued. "He used those cards to buy parts for the Mustang."

Kenzie added, "He kept it locked in the little garage behind the house. I was never allowed to drive it, but just in case he lost his keys, he gave me a set to hold onto. When I found out about the credit cards, I confronted him. He was furious that I dared to question him, but at the same time, he seemed to take great pleasure in letting me know that I was thirty thousand dollars in debt. So in a way, you see, I felt like that car belonged to me. So I...I took it."

Ryan said, "Since you are here with Clayton, it seems that you and Todd are no longer together. Is that accurate?"

"Very," said Kenzie. "I wish he would drop dead. He started texting me after I left, making threats. He said he would kill himself if I didn't bring his car back. He said his life depended on it. He said he would come after me if he had to."

Ryan tilted his head to one side. "If he committed credit card fraud, he's already in trouble with the law. Why don't you just let him take the car and get him off your back?"

Clayton drew a deep breath. Here it came. The part that Kenzie was obviously hesitant to talk about. He felt her eyes on him and squeezed her hand reassuringly. "Go ahead," he said, "tell him the rest of it. It's okay. He can't help us until he knows exactly what happened."

"Okay," said Kenzie. "I guess I went a little crazy. I realized that he was just using me and I had to get out of there. By then, I knew the whole thing with the house was a lie. In fact, the real estate company had discovered that we were living there and threatened to call the police if we didn't get out by noon. So I had to go. The only place I could think of was home. But I had no transportation. Then I found his spare set of keys in my purse. I went downstairs to the garage, found a hammer, broke the padlock, and took the car. At first, I thought I would just drive home in it and then leave it somewhere so he could find it. But by the time I got to Eagle's Toe, I don't know... it all came crashing down on me. My parents thought I was doing really well in Denver. They thought I had a house there that I was selling. I sort of exaggerated in my letters." She gave a little shrug of surrender. "They asked me to come home and help them because things weren't going well on the farm. They didn't know I was in debt. Thirty thousand may not sound like much to some people, but I was making minimum wage plus tip money. My parents were going to be horribly disappointed, and I felt like my life was ruined. I got angrier and angrier as I drove, and when I passed a sign for Old Quarry Road something in me just snapped. I took off the license plates, and I pushed the car over the edge of the quarry. That car was the only thing Todd ever really cared about, and at that moment, I just wanted to hurt him back."

When Kenzie fell silent, Clayton said softly, "Maybe that Perrier is a good idea."

Ryan pushed a button on his desk and said, "Jasmine? Could you bring us three bottles of Perrier, please?"

After a few moments, Jasmine entered with the water on the tray. She didn't ask any questions, and she pretended she didn't even see that Kenzie was weeping softly in her chair. She placed the tray on the desk, turned, and left. Ryan said quietly, "Don't worry. Jasmine never talks about what goes on in this office."

Kenzie wiped her eyes with the palm of one hand. Clayton reached for a tissue from the box on the corner of Ryan's desk and handed it to her.

Ryan opened the bottles of Perrier. As Clayton and Kenzie sipped their water, Ryan said, "Let's see. Your ex-boyfriend used you to get money through fake credit cards and lied to you about the house you thought you were buying. We also have a classic Mustang pushed off a cliff at the old quarry. We still haven't gotten to the money you found."

Clayton nodded. "That's coming up," he said. "Kenzie thought that Todd would just go away. After all, she did have the credit card fraud to hold over his head. But his texts and his threats kept getting more bold and obnoxious. The one that I saw was really awful. We decided that he seemed to need the car to insure his personal safety, but Kenzie never heard him rant like that before about the Mustang. So we began wondering if there might be something in the car that he wanted. And that's why we went to the quarry and searched it. To be honest, I half expected to find drugs in the car. But when we opened up the spare tire well, we found dozens of bundles of hundred dollar bills."

Ryan's eyes grew wide. "Dozens? Did you count it?"

"No. It was getting dark. We were using a flashlight, and if there was a night watchman, we thought he might see our light and wonder what we were doing. We had already heard a rumor about someone finding a new wreck out there. Evidently, they had spotted someone else's husk of a vehicle. But Kenzie was worried that the Mustang might be discovered any day, so we took the money out of the trunk and buried it in a slag heap."

Ryan looked at Kenzie and asked, "Any idea where he might have gotten that money?"

Kenzie shook her head. "He had a lot of bad friends," she said. "I know some of them did drugs. The hard stuff. Not marijuana. But I never trusted them. In fact, I was afraid of them. And as the months rolled by, I realized that Todd was no different than they were. Whatever they were into, Todd was into. But he never told me anything about what they did, where they went, or how they earned their money. So I have no idea."

Clayton said, "As soon as we left the quarry, we decided that the smartest move would be to get a lawyer in order to make sure that Kenzie had all the help she might need. What if it's drug money? Or what if he robbed a bank?"

Ryan asked, "Have you spent any of it?"

Clayton said, "No. I mean really, if the money is illegal, it might be marked or the serial numbers might be traceable. So we left it there. We didn't take anything."

At that moment, Kenzie made a strange little sound and dropped her Perrier all over the rug.

Chapter Fifteen

KENZIE GASPED. "I'M SO sorry!" She scrambled to pick up the bottle.

"No problem." Hutch grabbed a handful of tissues from the box on his desk and came around to sop up the wet spot. Once he was back in his chair, he asked, "Does that mean you've already spent some of the money?"

Kenzie shook her head vigorously. "No. Of course not." She looked away. Part of her wanted to say nothing, but what if Clayton was right? What if the money was ill-gotten gains and the authorities traced it back to her mother? She bowed her head, then looked apologetically at Clayton. "I took one of the bundles. I left it for my mother just this morning."

Clayton reassured her. "Your folks don't have a vehicle right now, so I doubt they'll be spending it soon."

"I'd hate to get them in trouble." She tightened her hold on her Perrier bottle, determined not to drop it again.

Ryan picked up his pencil and tapped the tablet. "Did you count it?"

"Yes." Kenzie looked from Clayton to Hutch and back. "That one bundle was over ten thousand dollars."

"Wow," said Clayton. "We moved how many? Twelve? Fifteen bundles?"

Hutch made notes. "So we're talking at least $120,000, if all the bundles were the same." He frowned. "Now we know why he's been sending threatening texts. May I see his messages?" He held out a hand. Reluctantly, Kenzie thumbed the screen to life and handed over her phone. She chewed her bottom lip as Hutch scrolled through the texts from Todd.

"Wow," he said at last. "They certainly escalated in a hurry. Why haven't you blocked his number?" He added notes to his legal pad, then handed the phone back.

Kenzie sighed. "Because when he's angry, he rants. And he tends to give himself away. He hasn't found me yet, but when he does, he'll probably send me another all-caps message saying he knows where I am. He can't help himself. He's not big on self-control. He wants to scare me. If I block him, I'll never know what he's thinking or where he is."

"Understood," said Hutch. "Don't erase those texts. They'll support a legal claim if you want to file for an injunction."

"Okay." She glanced sideways at Clayton. "What do we do now?"

Ryan spoke. "Does anyone else know about this?"

Kenzie's knuckles were white around the bottle. "Not unless someone stumbles over the Mustang."

Ryan raised a brow. "You mean, not *until* someone stumbles over it."

Clayton held up a finger. "Wait. I asked my cousin Thor to investigate this guy. He said he should have some info for me tomorrow."

Ryan jotted something down. "Your cousin is Thor Garrison?"

"Yes."

"Do you mind if I call him?"

"Fine by me," said Clayton. "Kenzie?"

"Yes, fine." She frowned at Clayton. "I don't remember you telling me you talked to your cousin."

Clayton reached for her hand. "I was worried about you," he said softly. "I wanted to know what kind of guy we're up against."

"We? I like that part." Kenzie smiled, then sobered. She wasn't sure if she was pleased or irritated by the rest of it. "He hangs out with a really bad crowd. Maybe I'm being silly, but there are at least three of them who really scare me. It's not just the black leather and the motorcycles. They got a kick out of staring at me so long and hard that I would run back into the house. Todd strutted around when I was present, but I saw him change his attitude many times after I went inside. I could see through the window that there were at least two of the gang that he kowtows to."

"A gang?" asked Ryan. "Do they have a name?"

Kenzie shrugged. "I don't know. They just felt like a gang to me. But they didn't wear emblems on their jackets like the Hell's Angels or anything."

Ryan nodded and jotted more on his pad. "Anything else you can tell me?"

Kenzie shrugged. "His phone number?"

Hutch's lips twitched in a tiny grin. "I got that when you showed me your phone. No permanent address?"

Kenzie sagged in her chair. "No." She glanced at Clayton. "We were squatting in that house. That's what the realtor called it when she discovered us. He was lying to me about everything."

Ryan opened his desk drawer and pulled out a pair of printed forms. He leaned forward and slid them toward Clayton and Kenzie. "I'd like you to fill these out so I have some basic information. While you're doing that, I'll write you a receipt for your retainer. Kenzie, don't forget to put down the address of that house you were living in. And I'll need your social security number."

Kenzie took a deep breath and willed her fears to leave on the exhale. "Will I go to jail for wrecking his stupid car?"

Ryan was already writing out a receipt. "Let me take care of that," he said. "Also, I'll start working on those fake credit cards."

"You mean, I won't have to pay them off?" Kenzie's voice was full of hope.

"This Todd fellow committed a crime by falsifying those applications and running up charges in your name without your knowledge. I should be able to help with that issue. If you can remember the names of the credit companies, add them to the bottom of your form. It will make my job easier."

"Whatever you say," she said, bending to fill out the form. Clayton had already finished his. When he slid it toward Ryan, he received the receipt for their retainers in exchange.

Ryan asked, "You haven't told your parents about these problems?"

Kenzie blushed. "No. I was afraid to. They'll be so disappointed in me."

Ryan shook his head. "They asked you to come home and help, and you came. That probably scored you a ton of points. With a little luck, we may get this cleared up before you have to tell them anything."

"What about the money I left for my mom?"

"She can hang onto it for a couple of days." He tapped his eraser against his desk. "Of course, she'll probably have a thousand questions about where it came from."

"I left a note telling her I'd finally received some of the money I was owed."

Ryan leaned back in his chair. "Well, what's done is done. Let me make some phone calls, do my lawyer magic, and see what I can find out."

"What about the money in the quarry?" asked Clayton.

Ryan clucked his tongue a few times. "Kenzie, how sure are you that Todd will let you know when he's coming?"

"Very sure. Should we move the cash?"

Ryan held up a hand. "Not yet. Even if someone finds the car, there's no reason for them to start digging around in slag piles. Let me figure out a few things first." He glanced at the forms they'd completed. "Good. I've got your phone numbers. You may hear from me later today. If not, definitely tomorrow."

They shook hands all around.

Kenzie felt like a new woman when they stepped out onto the sidewalk. "I know this isn't over," she said, "but thanks to you, I feel like there's hope for the first time in months. How can I ever repay you?"

Clayton put an arm around her shoulders and pulled her close. "Consider it a gift."

Kenzie kissed his cheek. "You are amazing."

Clayton grinned as he opened the Mercedes door for her. Then he said, "You ain't seen nothing yet. I have a surprise for you."

♡

Clayton refused to say another word, even though Kenzie pelted him with questions and guesses as he drove. When he pulled into Brady's Garage, she stopped talking.

"We're here."

Kenzie pinned him with a suspicious glance. "Clayton Masters, what have you done?"

Clayton shrugged. "I just had a little talk with Brady Felton. No big deal. You coming?" He smiled at her.

Kenzie opened her own door and slammed it hard. "Clayton! I only make ten dollars an hour. That's not enough to cover a car payment." She clutched her purse and lowered her voice. "I can't afford a vehicle right now."

"We'll see." He cupped her cheek with the palm of his hand. "Let's just go talk to Brady. That won't hurt anything." He opened the door to the office for her.

Inside, Brady looked up from his computer screen. "Clayton! Good to see you. Morning, Kenzie. Or is it noon already?"

"Almost," said Clayton. "Is it ready?"

"Not yet, but most likely it will be by, say, Monday afternoon? About the time Kenzie gets off work."

"Is what ready?" Kenzie looked from one to the other. "What have you two done?"

Clayton grinned. "Brady, would you like to do the honors?"

Brady looked like the cat that ate the canary. "It's a pleasure." He led the way through the waiting room to the door to the garage. "We can go through here. It's out on the lot." He talked as he walked. "You've been away to school, Kenzie, so you may not know this, but when my uncle died and left me this shop, there were a lot of loose ends to deal with. One of the reasons I decided to stay in Eagle's Toe was the fact that a number of locals stepped up to help me through that first year. And your father was one of them."

"He always believed in helping his neighbors," said Kenzie. She looked a question at Clayton.

He just smiled and nodded for her to follow Brady.

They stopped by a gray Ford F350. Brady patted the hood. "I've been repairing this truck in my spare time. Usually, I rebuild Volkswagens. The old ones. But I couldn't resist this challenge. A guy from Pueblo was off-roading with it, and he messed it up pretty bad. The transmission was limping along, and I had to do a rebuild on the engine. He decided he didn't want to pay for the repairs when he saw my estimate, so we settled on a price, and he signed the pink slip over to me. It's a six-year-old 6.4 liter V8 Turbo Diesel crew cab, can carry hay or haul a trailer, whatever you need around the farm."

Clayton watched Kenzie examine the truck as Brady described its features. Her desire for the vehicle was obvious.

When Brady finished, Kenzie crossed her arms. "Okay, give me the bad news. How much?"

Brady glanced at Clayton, who cleared his throat and held his palms up as if to stave off Kenzie's reaction. "Your parents need transportation. I love driving for you, but they have two dead trucks and no way to get around. I put a thousand down on this for you."

Kenzie's eyes widened. "I can't let you do that."

"Why not? Look, Kenzie, some day, I'm going to come into some money. Serious money. Okay? Meanwhile, just for breathing, I get an allowance. If I can send four thousand a month to support orphanages in China, I can make your truck payments. Until, you know, you get on your feet. It's okay."

Kenzie's mouth dropped open.

"It's a gift," said Clayton.

Kenzie shook her head in disbelief. "I'm speechless."

"I'll pick you up Monday afternoon at work, and I'll bring you over here so you can drive your truck home. How's that?"

For a nanosecond, she looked disappointed. "I suppose it's not fair to have you driving me back and forth."

Clayton smiled. "Actually, I love doing that. This truck is for your parents. They needed you to help them out, and this is a great way to start."

Kenzie's eyes glistened with tears. Before Clayton knew what was coming, she threw her arms around his neck and kissed him deeply. When the kiss ended, she pressed her palms against his chest. "How will I ever repay you?"

"It's a gift, remember?" It came out a whisper because he could barely breathe after her kiss.

"This will be a huge shot in the arm for my folks. Thank you so much. Brady, you, too."

"Your dad was there for me when I needed help," he said. "Glad to return the favor."

Kenzie wiped away a tear and nodded. "This is so overwhelming. I never realized how many wonderful friends my parents have."

Clayton breathed a sigh of relief. "Excellent. Truck problem solved. Oh. There is one thing."

Kenzie eyed him sideways. "What?"

"The Garrison barbecue tomorrow? Please come with me and promise me that at the end of the day, you'll still love me."

Kenzie laughed. "Why wouldn't I?"

"Because my aunt Polly is probably going to give you the third degree."

"No problem," said Kenzie, leaning against him. "I've got a lawyer."

♡

Kenzie felt she was floating on air for the rest of the day. She slipped one arm around Clayton's waist and tucked two fingers into the waist of his jeans, while he draped an arm around her shoulders as if it were glued there.

She knew she ate lunch because he let her direct him to The Nest, the mom-and-pop burger joint where she and her high school friends used to spend hours hanging out. He confessed he'd been there before but would not have found it again on a bet. She told him about their contests to see who could make a large Coke last the longest, and he challenged her to see if she could make her fries last longer than his. After fifteen minutes, he gave up and scarfed the rest of his down. Then she took pity on him and told him she only liked them hot.

"Once that hot-fry window closes," she said, "I might as well toss them out."

"Well, thanks for explaining. I was beginning to think my father was right and I had no will power."

So she definitely ate lunch, but other than the fries, she couldn't remember what she had. All she could focus on were Clayton's kiwi-green eyes and that marvelous, sensuous mouth. Now that she knew what it felt like to kiss those lips, she couldn't stop thinking about it.

After lunch, they went to the Gallery, and Clayton insisted she pick out another porcelain figurine to go with her cowgirl and her pony. She spotted one right away, a blond cowboy holding his black hat against one leg of his jeans while a black-and-white dog leaned against the other one, looking up at him adoringly.

"This one is perfect," she murmured. "He even has green eyes."

At three-thirty, she reminded him reluctantly, "I have to go home and do the chores."

Clayton pulled her into another warm kiss. When they ran out of air and had to part, he sighed, "Okay. But don't forget, I'm picking you up early in the morning. I want to show you off to my brother and my cousins."

They spent another ten minutes in the Mercedes, parked in front of her house, practicing the perfect kiss. When the dogs started barking outside the car, she moaned, "Oh darn. I guess we'll have to arrange another time for practice."

Clayton nuzzled her neck and said, "I'll make sure we get more tomorrow."

Kenzie cradled her new figurine in one hand as she exited the car. She stood and watched him drive away until she lost sight of the black spot as it sped down the highway.

She reached down and rubbed Cotton's ears. "I'm definitely in love," she said, looking the dog in the eye. "Can you stand to be around me?"

He whined and licked her hand, then spun in circles. She laughed. "Okay, inside. I'll feed you first."

Once in the living room, she again had a distinct feeling of impending doom. It was too quiet, and the drapes were closed again. Her mother's voice startled her.

"I'm here, Kenzie. Just resting in your dad's old chair."

Kenzie tucked the figurine in her pocket and went to her mother's side. "Are you all right? You look exhausted again."

"I'll be fine." Marigold smiled weakly. Her eyes sparkled when she announced, "Your dad is feeling much better. We already had a light dinner. Soup and crackers. You don't mind fending for yourself after chores, do you?"

"Of course not." Kenzie squeezed her mother's hand. "Would you like me to put the TV on?"

"Sure. Find that old movie channel. I don't want to listen to the news. It makes me crazy."

Kenzie took the remote and found her mother's movie channel. "Here. You take it. You can change it if you want. I'll go feed the animals."

"Did you have a good time?" Marigold's voice seemed strangely soft, as if all the air had leaked out of the bellows.

"It was wonderful," said Kenzie. Then she cocked her head to one side. "Did you find your surprise in the fridge?"

Marigold smiled so wide, her eyes squinted shut. "You're such a wonderful child. I left it right where I found it. It's safe there. Now we can replace the truck."

"I've already taken care of that," said Kenzie. "I'll be driving it home Monday after work."

Her mother's eyes opened wide. "Oh, you darling girl." She touched Kenzie's arm lightly. Kenzie frowned at how cold her mother's hand was.

"I'm going to get you a blanket, Mom. You're getting chilly down here. Let me know when you want to go to bed, and I'll help you up the stairs."

Marigold brushed away her concern. "I'll be fine. I'm just worn out from taking care of your father. Maybe the blue blanket you washed yesterday?"

Kenzie smiled. "You got it."

After delivering the blanket, Kenzie went out to do the chores. After the animals were fed, she made herself a half-sandwich and marveled at how delicious tuna fish could be when a person was in love. She ended up splitting the last bite between the dogs. When she checked on her mother, Marigold was sound asleep. Kenzie decided not to wake her. Instead, she went upstairs, said good night to her father, and was pleasantly surprised when he asked about the animals.

"I'll be up and about tomorrow," he said. "Your mother mentioned you'll be going out with your gentleman friend again. I'll get up and do the morning chores. You can just get yourself ready for Clayton. How's that?"

"Thanks, Dad." She kissed him on the cheek and was relieved to find his skin warm and dry. "Mom fell asleep downstairs, so if you hear noises in the night, it's probably her coming to bed."

She retired to her room and set the porcelain cowboy on the nightstand next to the cowgirl and her pony. She spent an hour letting them have a pretend conversation, something she hadn't done since she was twelve. At last, she put on her pajamas and lay in bed, thinking about Clayton. She plugged her phone in to charge and turned it off before her mood could be ruined by any more messages from what's-his-face. Then she laughed. She hadn't thought about Todd or the rest of her troubles since lunch.

She dreamed about buying a house with Clayton using the money from the slag heap. It had magically grown into a million dollars, and it all seemed perfectly reasonable. They were arranging their living room furniture when there was a thud at the door of her dream living room. She opened it, and Todd stood there, soaked in gasoline. When he lit the match, Kenzie woke up with a shout and bolted straight up in bed.

It took an hour to calm down enough to erase that awful image. She could hear her mother's voice in her head, warning her, "Don't count your chickens before they hatch." No kidding.

Chapter Sixteen

SUNDAY MORNING, KENZIE was relieved to see that her father was feeling well enough to help with the chores. Even though he'd told her he would do them all, she couldn't bear to let him, not on his first day out of bed. He was even in a good mood. He whistled a tune as he tossed flakes of hay to the cows. Kenzie insisted on doing the heavy lifting though. She had to move some bags of pig food and goat chow, and there was always manure to cleanup. Even so, it did her heart good to see the pink flush on her father's cheeks and have him actually smile at her as they worked. He never was much of a talker. But that was okay. She was just so happy that he was not lying in bed.

Her mother looked happy, too. She had fixed a modest breakfast, most likely so John's lagging appetite wasn't as obvious. She'd prepared one egg apiece and toasted homemade bread and a few slices of bacon. By the time Kenzie checked her phone—it was way too early for Todd to be up and threatening her—her mom and dad were chatting like old times. It filled Kenzie's heart with joy and hope. She had chosen to wear a full-length dark green velvet dress.

"Dad, are you sure it's okay if I go to the barbecue?" she asked. "If you need me, I can stay home."

"No, I won't hear of it." Her father's voice was not quite as hale and hearty as he appeared, but it had more energy behind it then she had heard all week. "I don't want you to hang around here when you've got a young man waiting to take you out. You've been working all week long, doing all the

116

chores here and then going into town and working at the Feed and Grain. You deserve at least one day off. I'll be fine. Besides, your mother is here."

Marigold still looked tired, but she agreed. "Your father's right."

"I didn't hear you go upstairs last night, Mom."

Marigold grumbled, "That's because I didn't. Can you believe how lazy I'm getting in my old age? I slept the whole night right there in that chair." She shook her head in disgust. Then she lightened her tone and said, "My, my, you look wonderful in that dress. I was afraid you didn't like it."

"Maybe you got that impression because of the fit I threw before prom," said Kenzie. "I don't know if I ever told you, but I was the envy of every girl there that night. They were all shiny and spangly in their off-the-shoulder imitation bridal gowns, and there I was in this hand-sewn dark green velvet dress. I love the lace at the wrists and neckline. It makes me feel Victorian and more than a little haughty." She tipped her nose in the air and did a slow turn.

Marigold laughed silently. "And you found your lace-up boots. You are a vision, Kenzie."

"Thanks, Mom."

Marigold gave her a secret smile. When John left the room to wash his hands, she whispered, "I'm not going to tell your father about the money yet. I want to think about how best to use it."

"That sounds fine to me," said Kenzie softly. After all, if the money had been stolen, spending it might get her folks in trouble. She was even glad she wouldn't bring the Ford F350 home until after work Monday. That gave Ryan Hutch and Thor until Tuesday to figure out whether she could keep it or not. If things went to hell in a hand basket, she couldn't expect Clayton to fulfill his promise about the truck payment. What if the police traced her connection to Todd? Would whatever he had done to acquire the cash then be her crime by association? But for now, she shook off those worries as she watched her parents looking more normal than she'd seen them since her return.

It didn't take long before her father was looking peaked. Marigold put a brave face on it. "Well, John, you were sick in bed for a week. You can't expect to jump right back into your usual routine. I think it would make a lot of sense for you to put your feet up in the easy chair and watch a football game. I warmed it up for you last night. If Kenzie isn't back in time for chores, I'll fill in for her."

"Thanks, Mom. I promise I won't be out too late. But I don't have any idea how long these family things last with the Garrisons."

John squinted at her. "Garrisons? I thought this fellow's name was Masters."

"That's right," said Kenzie. "He's related on Polly Garrison's side. Her maiden name was Masters."

Marigold looked pleased.

"I think he really likes me," said Kenzie. *Otherwise, why would he hang around after seeing what she'd done to Todd's car? And how many guys would take it in stride if their new girl friend needed a lawyer?* "I like him, too. A lot."

"Good," said Marigold. "See? If you hadn't come home, you never would have met him."

The dogs barked out front.

"That must be him now," said Kenzie.

John had recovered some of his natural grumpiness. "Is he going to sit out there and honk for you?"

No sooner were the words out of his mouth than the doorbell rang.

Kenzie beamed. "Hardly, Dad." She went to open the door.

Clayton held a dozen pink roses. "I hope you like the color," he said. "Someone told me every color of rose had a special meaning, but when I asked for an explanation, he admitted he didn't really know."

"They're lovely," gushed Kenzie. "Come on in. We'll let my folks enjoy them while we're gone." She led the way to the kitchen.

Clayton went to shake John's hand before the older man had time to struggle to his feet. "So nice to see you up and around, sir."

John grunted his approval.

Kenzie kept touching Clayton's arm, then pulling her hand back, wondering how much affection she should show in front of her parents. Clayton solved the problem for her by slipping his arm around her waist.

"You look gorgeous in that dress," he said. "Is that velvet?"

"Yes," said Kenzie. "I hope it's not too formal for the barbecue."

Clayton beamed. "Are you kidding? My aunt Polly is going to be so impressed."

"My mother made it for me."

Marigold waved away the compliment. "I used to sew a lot when I was younger."

Clayton said tenderly, "It's a work of art, fit for a princess."

John humphed, but his eyes twinkled. "You two go on and have a good time. We'll hold down the fort here."

Kenzie leaned over to kiss his forehead. She frowned momentarily. His skin was clammy again. But then, he was still recovering from whatever that nasty bug was. She gave her mother a peck on the cheek. "I'll see you both later."

♡

Clayton wished he could skip the family barbecue and whisk Kenzie off to some exotic location. But whisking on the first date might be misinterpreted as kidnapping. He suppressed a smile and wondered if this was technically a second date since they had spent all day Saturday together.

"Before we get to my cousin's place, I should tell you that Thor and Ryan were working on our problem all yesterday afternoon and evening."

"No movie?"

"Nope."

"Poor Jasmine."

Clayton humphed.

"What?" asked Kenzie.

"You're neck deep in problems and you're feeling sorry for Jasmine missing a movie." He shook his head and added softly, "You're one in a million."

Kenzie smiled and turned away to look out the window. "Thanks."

"I'm glad your dad is feeling better."

"Me, too." She cast a worried glance his way. "My mom sure is tired. It's been a really long week for her."

"Is your phone on? In case they call?"

Kenzie put her hand to her mouth. "Oh! I left it on the nightstand. I forgot all about it. I don't even remember if I turned it on or not."

"Maybe that's a good thing." Clayton took her hand and pulled it to his lips for a kiss.

Kenzie looked happy, and that pleased Clayton no end.

"Don't worry," she said. "They have a land line, and a list of phone numbers for everyone in town."

"Okay," he said as he pulled up in front of Thor and Ashley's luxury cabin. "Here we are. There's Austin's car, so he and Erin are already here."

"Gosh, they start early."

Clayton laughed. "When we were kids, everyone would arrive the night before and sleep over. Now that we're grown, we've given that up. But Thor is the only one with kids so far, so I suspect the old custom will return when we have a passel of little cousins running around." He turned off the engine. "I hope you like kids. Thor has two little ones."

Rocky slammed his big paws against Kenzie's window and barked loud and long.

"Sorry about that," said Clayton. "Don't be afraid."

Kenzie laughed. "Are you kidding? I have goats bigger than him." She started to open her car door.

"Wait for Thor," said Clayton. "I don't want Rocky's paws all over that beautiful dress."

Kenzie gave him a look that made him wish they didn't have to spend the day with relatives. Two spots of color rose on her cheeks, and she said, "You are the most thoughtful man I've ever met."

Clayton stayed close to Kenzie as he introduced her to Thor, Ashley, and the babies. Austin and Erin were delighted to meet her as well. His heart warmed at the sight of her playing with little Odin, and he was surprised when she asked to hold Freya.

"Oh, you like kids," he said.

"Sure," said Kenzie. "They're as cute as baby goats and cleaner than baby pigs. What's not to love? With my siblings all in the service, and planning to make careers of it, I may be my parents' only hope for grandchildren." She laughed softly and wiped drool off Freya's chin.

Clayton looked around the kitchen and gazed across the great room. "Hey Thor, I don't see Axel and Taylor. Are they coming?"

Thor paused before going out on the deck to the barbecue. "Axel said they'd be here. But you know how much he loves those reindeer. And Taylor hates the alpacas, so he probably has to tend to them by himself. It might take him a while to straighten all that out, feed the animals, and so on."

Kenzie rocked Freya gently in her arms and piped up, "Oh, Taylor doesn't hate them all that much. She confessed at work that they're starting to grow on her. But she adores the reindeer."

"Where's Aunt Polly?" Clayton went to hold the door open for Thor.

"She sleeps late. She'll get here around noon."

"Can I give you a hand?"

"Sure. I think Ashley and Erin wanted to take Kenzie upstairs and show her the nursery."

"You built on?"

Thor gave a wry grin. "Ashley says I'm like Sarah Winchester. She just kept building and building until she died. Besides, Ash wanted a space upstairs near our bedroom for the babies. I thought we told you about that last year?"

Clayton caught Kenzie's eye. She looked completely at home, and Erin and Ashley were complimenting her on her dress. Ashley was insisting on putting a blanket between Freya and the velvet. Kenzie flashed Clayton a grin, and he relaxed and followed Thor out on the deck.

♡

For Kenzie, the morning sped by. She adored the two little ones, and loved the nursery.

"Wow," she said, awestruck. "I would love to have a nursery like this— a play area, a sleeping alcove, and look at all those toys! I don't suppose you'd consider adopting me?"

Ashley grinned and lowered herself into a baby-blue rocker. "You would have to walk on your knees for a few years," she teased.

"Definitely worth it." Kenzie deposited Freya gently in Ashley's arms.

Erin bounced as she talked, as if trying to make herself taller. "Austin says his brother is really in love with you."

Kenzie blushed. "I'm sort of enamored of him, too. He's so handsome. That incredible mouth...."

Erin giggled. "It runs in the family. Austin seems quiet and nerdy to other people, but once you get to know him, you realized that he's very deep."

"And nerdy," teased Ashley.

Erin nodded. "Deep and nerdy. So true. And a great photographer."

Kenzie moved slowly about the room, running her fingers over cribs and baby swings and chests-of-drawers. "Are you planning a family, Erin?"

"Someday. Maybe after I get tired of teaching. Austin wants me to be able to stay at home with the baby, when the time comes. Oh! You should see the nursery at Axel and Taylor's house! Axel's dad sent them an entire eighteen-wheeler packed with nursery stuff. But so far, no kids."

Kenzie murmured, "Wow. Nothing like being prepared, I guess."

"What about you?" asked Ashley. "Are you thinking long-term about Clayton? Are you two getting serious?"

Kenzie dropped her head shyly. "I'm definitely serious about him. I hope he feels the same. He's helping me clean up some trouble I left behind in Denver. And he's been chauffeuring me back and forth from work and buying me gifts and roses." She sighed, then realized Erin and Ashley were watching her closely. "Sorry," she said, shaking off her reverie. "I guess you can tell that I adore him."

"That's a good thing," said Erin. "Austin will be thrilled. Have you met his father yet? Austin always puts me on the phone after they speak their allotted fifty words to each other."

"Fifty words?" Kenzie asked.

Ashley said, "She's exaggerating. More like twenty-five."

Erin laughed. "Well, Austin gets his lack of loquaciousness from his dad."

Kenzie smiled. "I'm glad Clayton is a talker. Gee, do you think we should be doing something in the kitchen?"

Ashley shook her head. "Barbecue. Man's work. Let them handle it. Goodness knows, I have tons of opportunities to be the cook and bottle washer."

They chatted like old friends, and Kenzie was amazed at how comfortable she felt around so much wealth. Of course, Erin and Ashley had come from modest backgrounds, just like her, so the three of them hit it off right away.

Before she realized it, the morning was gone. From the window, they spotted Axel and Taylor driving up.

"I suppose we should go downstairs," Ashley said reluctantly.

Just then, a woman's strident voice floated up from below. "Where are you girls? I don't want to miss anything."

Ashley said quietly, "Okay, fun time's over. Here comes my mother-in-law."

Kenzie let that sink in for a moment. Clayton had warned her about Polly. She made a mental note to ask Ashley some questions when she got a chance.

When they reached the bottom of the stairs, Polly was greeting Axel and Taylor at the front door. Thor stuck his head in from the deck and called out, "Steaks are ready! Hey, Axel, great timing."

The food was delicious. Kenzie surprised herself by eating an entire steak. The meal started out on the deck, but soon everyone took their plates into the big kitchen because the weather was turning colder and grayer.

"Snow tonight?" asked Erin.

Kenzie responded like the local girl she was. "Not yet. Sky's too dark. When it turns white, we'll have snow."

By the time dessert rolled around, Kenzie could tell that Polly was looking for an opportunity to corner her for a conversation. Just about then, Clayton took Kenzie's elbow and said quietly, "It's time to escape for a moment and get an update from Thor. He just hung up from talking to Ryan right before the steaks were ready."

But Polly was having none of it. "Oh no, you boys go on and do your man thing. I want to talk to Kenzie. I need to get to know this young lady." She took hold of Kenzie's other elbow and pulled in the opposite direction.

Clayton's eyebrows rose, and he glared at his aunt. Kenzie adopted a gracious tone. "Don't worry, Clayton. I would love to talk to Polly. I need to learn a little bit about your family. Don't you agree? You can fill me in on things later. Meanwhile, I promise to ask Polly for very embarrassing stories about your childhood."

Polly laughed with delight. "Y'all come on, girl," she said, letting every bit of her Texas upbringing show in her voice. "I have some things to tell you that you will not believe."

Kenzie made an eek face, shrugged apologetically at Clayton, and let Polly pull her off to one side of the living room. Clayton nodded and silently mouthed the words, "I'll fill you in later."

Ashley and Erin bundled the children up against the cold and escorted them outside. Kenzie could hear little Odin screeching with joy as his tiny feet thumped back and forth on the deck. Austin was tagging along with his brother, and although Kenzie was beginning to wonder how many people were going to know about her problems, she decided that she really couldn't expect Clayton to exclude Austin.

As a result, the great room was empty except for Polly and Kenzie. Polly steered her to the sofa and they sat down. After an awkward pause, Kenzie blurted, "It's so nice to meet some of Clayton's relatives."

Polly raised one eyebrow. "Now are you just saying that? Or do you feel true affection for my nephew?"

Kenzie was taken aback. She tilted her head to one side. "Excuse me?"

Polly waved a hand in the air, and two Chihuahuas rushed toward her. She picked them up and put them on her lap. "I'm just trying to find out if your intentions toward Clayton are genuine."

Kenzie frowned. "Shouldn't it be my parents asking Clayton these questions?"

Polly laughed, but there was no real feeling behind it. She pinned Kenzie with a calculating look. "I just want to know whether you're the special girl Clayton says you are or just a very clever opportunist. Lots of women in this world would do anything to marry someone about to become a billionaire."

Kenzie's eyes opened wide, and her mouth followed suit. After several seconds, she shook her head like someone coming out of a trance and stared at Polly as if the woman were insane. "I'm not sure what you're talking about," she said. "Clayton has told me that he does receive money from his father every month, but he doesn't expect to see any funds coming other than that. He's a very generous man, and I'm impressed with how he handles the income that he has. And he's extremely concerned that his father thinks he's a playboy. My feelings for Clayton have nothing to do with money or the lack thereof. He came into my life when I thought I would never trust a man again, and he has shown me that just because I had one horrible experience doesn't mean that all men are creeps. I would love Clayton..." She paused, considering her words carefully. "...yes, I said it. I love Clayton with all my heart, and I would continue to love him if he were stone-cold broke. Does that help answer your question?" She tried to stay calm but realized her tone was growing more defensive with every word. She added, "I'm sorry, but I've never had anyone question my motivations before."

Polly patted Kenzie's knee. "I believe you," she said. "You speak with conviction, and I pride myself on being able to read people well. So I hope you'll forgive me for speaking so plainly. It's just that... well, my brother, Plano, has been talking to me on the phone a lot this week because Clayton is avoiding him. And I can understand why because sometimes Plano can be really irritating. He's a stubborn man and used to getting his way. He worries about his children and he wants the best for them, and when there's a lot of money involved, some women's motivations are not as pure as yours. If you get my drift."

Kenzie's brow creased in puzzlement. "I'm not sure I understand exactly what you're saying," she said. "I'm happy that you trust my motives, but are you asking me this because Clayton's father is worried that I might take advantage of his son?"

"Well, it has happened in the past," said Polly. "In fact, I was worried about Ashley when I first met her. After all, she was the one who told me that she and Thor were engaged. She just took over and pushed out his old girlfriend and I was worried that she was after his money. Granted, his daddy and I, as well as my brother, Plano, have much bigger bank accounts, and a lot more holdings than the kids do, but there will come a day when all that settles on our children. So we do worry a little bit when someone new comes into the family circle."

Kenzie was pleased to hear herself described as someone in the family circle, but at the same time, she was horrified at the thought that Clayton's family suspected her of being interested only in his future fortune. Whatever that might be. She busied herself by smoothing the wrinkles out of her long velvet skirt and asked, "Am I to assume that Clayton's father thinks I'm faking my feelings for his son?"

Polly tossed her head as if that were a ludicrous question. "Oh no, sweetie, Plano is quite certain that there are many things about Clayton that you adore. He's just worried that they have dollar signs attached. It wouldn't be the first time that one of our children tried to fake a marriage in order to get their inheritance a few years earlier than planned."

Kenzie was horrified. She put a hand to her mouth. She thought she might throw up. "Are you telling me that you think Clayton is courting me because he wants to fake a marriage with me and trick his father into giving him his inheritance?"

"Well, I hope not," said Polly. "You, however, strike me as a bright young lady and maybe it's good that I mentioned this, because I would hate for you to be deceived by Clayton."

Kenzie felt the world slipping away beneath her. She became aware of a pain growing around her heart. It spread outward to her rib cage until she couldn't breathe. She stood up and faced Polly. "I must say, I've learned a lot today. I suppose I should be grateful for your heads-up about Clayton. After all, it's better that I know he doesn't return my affection now, before I become more attached to him. You can tell him for me that he doesn't have to worry about his inheritance. And you can tell that to his father as well."

The sound of male laughter drifted in from the kitchen as the others returned from the deck. Kenzie turned to leave just as Clayton approached her. She saw him glance at Polly with a question in his eyes and then look at her with an even bigger question on his face. "Kenzie? What's wrong? What happened?"

Kenzie pulled herself up to her full height, straightened her shoulders, and said, "I'm not interested in a fake relationship, Clayton. If that's what this is all about, I'll just handle my problems on my own. Thank you very much. Enjoy the truck you bought." She turned and stomped out of the house, slamming the door behind her.

Out on the porch, she realized that a dramatic exit was impossible when one did not have transportation of one's own. Since she didn't have keys to the Mercedes, she crossed her arms and began pacing back and forth beside the car. What was she going to do? How could Polly say such things? She hadn't asked Clayton for any help at all. Everything had been freely offered. Or had it? Was he really looking for someone to help him fool his father into thinking that he was settling down so he could get his inheritance? She couldn't even believe that the word inheritance had been part of their conversation. The only thing Kenzie ever expected to inherit was a farm that she and her siblings would have to secure with a bank loan to afford the taxes. Her inheritance would come in the form of goats and pigs and whatever cattle her father had left. Her inheritance would be scrabbling to keep body and soul together, just like her family had been doing for generations.

She stopped pacing when she heard the front door of the house close again. She turned around to see Clayton rushing toward her. Uncertain about how to react, she bolted down the driveway. Clayton ran to catch up.

"Kenzie, what did Polly say to you? Never mind. I think I know what she said. This is all my father's fault. He has this crazy idea that I'm looking for a fake bride so I can trick his lawyers into letting me have more money. I don't care about that. I don't care about my father's money. You have to believe me." She kept walking and he kept pace beside her, trying to convince her. "Kenzie, please stop and let me talk to you. Please. I love you. I love you because of who and what you are. Because you're the most beautiful woman I've ever met. Because the first moment I saw you, I suddenly realized that nothing else mattered."

Kenzie stopped at last. She turned to face him, her hands balled into fists, and sputtered, "How could you lie to me? Haven't I had enough pain in my life already? How could you take advantage of me at my weakest moment?"

Clayton took her shoulders in his hands and held her gently. "Kenzie, my feelings for you are genuine. Don't you understand? My aunt Polly has a reputation for saying crazy things at the worst time. I'm telling you from the bottom of my heart how I feel. I adore you. I never want to be with another woman as long as I live. I want to help you. I want you to be able to move forward without worrying about the things that happened in your past. Please believe me." He pulled her a bit closer, and she did not resist. Their lips were inches apart. Kenzie could feel Clayton's breath on her lips. A moment later, he kissed her warmly.

The pain around Kenzie's heart began to dissipate, lifting like a dark cloud pushed by the winds of promise. The pain was gone, and now her heart fluttered on wings of joy. When the kiss ended, she threw her arms around his neck. "Oh Clayton, I was so upset. I was scared that you didn't really love me. How could she say those things?"

"I guess now would be a good time to tell you that some people in my family are overly dramatic."

Kenzie laughed out loud. Relief made her giddy. "Oh my God, Clayton. I thought I'd just lost you. I thought everything was over. I couldn't bear to not have you in my life." But she was still worried. "Does your aunt Polly really think that I'm after your money?"

Clayton smoothed her cheek with the palm of his hand. He pushed her hair back behind her ear and stared lovingly into her eyes. At that moment Kenzie thought her heart would explode from happiness.

He said, "Aunt Polly just talks. She talks all the time. Every time my father tells her something or gives her an idea about something, she goes off on a tear. She's normally a kind, good-hearted woman. She's been very sweet to me since my mother died. But you've got to ignore anything she said to you about our relationship. Can you do that? Can you accept the fact that I truly love you for who you are?"

Kenzie pressed her face against his neck and held him tight. When his arms wrapped warmly around her, she let all her concerns float away. "I'm so glad, Clayton. Because I love you, too. I don't know what I would do without you. You've made such a difference in my life. I just want to be with you forever."

Clayton hugged her even tighter and murmured in her ear, "That's exactly what I want, too, Kenzie. I want us to be together forever. I didn't even tell my father about you because of his suspicious mind." He stepped back for a second, letting them both breathe. "In fact, when he said that to me—"

Kenzie was horrified. "He actually accused you directly of trying to fake a marriage?"

Clayton took her hands and kissed her fingers. "Yes," he said, "that's the kind of suspicious mind he has."

"What did you say to him?"

Clayton gave her one of his mischievous looks and said, "I told him I would never let him meet you if that's what he thought was going on. I told him we'll give him a call after our first child is born."

Kenzie laughed with delight, threw her arms around his neck, and kissed him deeply. "Oh, Clayton, I love you so much."

The special moment ended when Austin came running from the house. "Kenzie! The hospital just called! Your parents are in the ER!"

Chapter Seventeen

CLAYTON DROVE LIKE A maniac from Thor's cabin to Fineman Memorial. He tossed the keys to the valet parking attendant as Kenzie broke into a run toward the ER entrance.

Once inside, she danced from one foot to another in front of the reception desk. Half a dozen people sat in the waiting room, their faces tight with tension. A harried-looking nurse was talking on the phone behind the desk. At last she hung up and Kenzie asked, "Mr. and Mrs. Shane? I got a call that Mr. and Mrs. Shane are here in the ER?"

The nurse maintained her composure. "And you are...?"

"I'm their daughter, Kenzie Shane."

The nurse lifted a different phone and spoke to someone in the back. "Kenzie Shane is here to see her parents." A moment later she hung up and said to Kenzie, "Go right through those doors, dear. A nurse can direct you from there."

Kenzie could barely contain herself as she pushed the double doors open. She could feel Clayton right behind her, and it was a great comfort. A nurse in blue scrubs waved her forward. "Come this way," she said. "Your parents are in a treatment room." She led the way through another set of doors to a long row of cubicle rooms that provided a small amount privacy. "Here you go. Your mother is scheduled for surgery in the morning." She smiled briefly, turned on her heel, and left.

"My mother?!"

John Shane was standing next to the bed, holding Marigold's hand. She was festooned with tubes and an oxygen mask, and surrounded by an array of incomprehensible machines. Her eyes were closed and her face was very pale. John looked exhausted.

"Dad! When they called, I thought—"

He nodded. "I know, I know. Turns out I've been walking around with pneumonia. They already gave me antibiotics."

"But Mom...?"

John patted Marigold's hand and pulled Kenzie into a hug. "Your mother has had a heart attack."

"Oh my God!" Kenzie hugged him back. She peered around his shoulder. "Is she awake?"

"She floats in and out. They've stabilized her, but the cardiologist says she needs surgery. First thing in the morning." He acknowledged Clayton and shook his hand. "Thanks for bringing her over. I couldn't call direct because she left her cell phone at home." He released Kenzie and pulled her phone out of his pocket. It looked like a doll accessory in his large, calloused hand. "It kept dinging and dinging," he said. "Your mother insisted on going upstairs and seeing if there was an emergency." He shook his head. "That last climb up the stairs was too much. She came out of your room with the phone in her hand and collapsed on the landing. I called 911 and here we are." He gave Kenzie the phone. She slipped it in her pocket.

"What kind of surgery does she need?" she asked, glancing toward her mother as she spoke. "Why is she so pale? Did she ever complain of chest pain?" She unconsciously reached for Clayton's hand.

John shook his head. "No chest pains ever. But the doctor said that's not uncommon for women. She's been so tired for the last month or so. Even before you came home." He dropped his head. "Wearing herself out tending to me. I should have done what she asked and went to the doctor. Walking pneumonia. That's why I've felt so lousy. This is my fault."

"Oh no, Dad, I'm sure that's not true."

John struggled to compose his features. At last, he said gruffly, "The staff is going to put an extra bed in her room so I can stay with her. They won't do surgery until morning. They said she needs something...stents? Is that the word?"

Kenzie nodded. "How many?"

John shrugged and shook his head. "I'm sorry, baby. There was so much information flying, I couldn't catch it all."

Kenzie looked from her father to Clayton. "What should we do? Should we stay with Dad?"

Her father made the decision. "No, no, you go on home and get some sleep. But if you want to come back in the morning and wait out the surgery with me, I'd appreciate it."

"Of course," said Kenzie. She looked a question at Clayton.

"Don't worry, Mr. Shane, I'll get her here."

A nurse bustled in to check the readouts on the machines attached to Marigold.

John hesitated. He took a long look at his wife, then said, "Let's step into the hall for a minute."

Kenzie and Clayton followed him.

John said quietly, "Clayton, I'd appreciate it if you'd stay at the house and look out for Kenzie while her mother is in the hospital."

Clayton looked surprised. "Well, sure, if you want me to."

Kenzie was puzzled and a tiny bit annoyed. "Dad, I'm a grown woman. I can take care of all the chores. I'll be fine."

"Under normal circumstances," said John, "I would agree. But...well, you better take a look at those last messages that came on your phone. The ones your mother read right before she collapsed. They were showing on that gadget when I took it from Marigold, but the screen's gone dark now. I don't want you staying alone, period. Just do this for me and don't argue." The brusqueness of his words was softened when he planted a kiss on Kenzie's forehead. "You go on, get home and feed the animals. Clayton, I'm counting on you."

The nurse left, and John resumed his vigil by Marigold's bed.

Kenzie hesitated, but Clayton took her hand and led her out of the ER. "Your mother will be okay," he said. "Modern medicine is amazing. A couple of stents, and she'll be like a new woman."

He tipped the valet for retrieving the Mercedes.

Kenzie didn't say a word until they were in the car. She pulled her phone and opened the message screen. Her eyes filled with tears and her chin trembled. She turned the phone toward Clayton and whispered, "This is why she had a heart attack."

♡

Clayton pulled over to the curb and took the phone. He scrolled through the last three messages that Todd had sent. They were openly threatening, full of profanity. The last one, however, was direct and to the point.

"I KNOW WHERE YOU ARE. I'M COMING TO MAKE YOU PAY. WATCH YOUR BACK."

Clayton drew a deep breath, exhaled, and turned off the phone. "No wonder your dad wants me to stay with you."

"What am I going to do?"

Clayton caressed her cheek. "What are *we* going to do," he corrected gently. "Don't worry. We'll stop at the Cattleman's so I can pick up my things, and then I'll amuse you by helping feed the animals."

Kenzie almost smiled.

"And once the chores are done, I'm going to make a few phone calls."

Seeing Clayton in her father's overalls and boots was definitely one way to lighten Kenzie's mood. After she hung her velvet dress lovingly in the closet, she donned her jeans and a plaid shirt, and headed down to the kitchen. The sight of Clayton made her laugh out loud. But her relief was fleeting, and by the time they finished the barn chores, she was weighed down once more with worry about her mother.

True to his word, once the animals were tended to, Clayton sat at the kitchen table and began making calls. He began with the nursing station at the hospital on the floor where Marigold had been taken to await surgery, so he could leave his cell phone number for John Shane and a message that Kenzie's phone had been turned off.

Next, he called Thor. "You know the town and the people," said Clayton. "Kenzie's too upset to think straight right now. But from what I've seen since I got here, Eagle's Toe is very fond of the Shane family. Maybe you could let a few of them know what's going on."

Thor said, "Of course. Tell Kenzie to hang in there. We're a small town but we have a world-class hospital. Have you talked to Ryan Hutch?"

"I was just about to do that. But first, are Austin and Erin still there?"

"No. They left about ten minutes ago. Axel and Taylor just left, as well. They may be headed your way."

Clayton sighed. "All right. I'll try them after I call Hutch. Did you learn anything more?"

"I had a colleague check out that house they were living in. A few locals mentioned that they'd seen Todd in the area, but not since yesterday. One of them thinks he's on the move because they haven't heard his motorcycle ripping up and down the streets today."

"He's definitely on the move," said Clayton. "He texted Kenzie that he was coming to get her."

"That's not good."

"No kidding."

Thor said, "You take care of Kenzie. I have a couple of ideas. I'll get back to you."

Clayton hung up the phone and stretched some of the tension out of his neck. "Will the dogs let us know if any strangers come around?"

Kenzie nodded. "They're old, but they still feel like they're on duty."

"Do your folks own any guns?"

"Yes. Dad used to go hunting a lot. I'll show you." She led him to a hideaway under the stairs. The door was only five feet tall so they had to duck to go inside. Kenzie pulled the chain on the light in the ceiling and revealed two gun racks and boxes of ammo. There were also two hardwood cases, each containing a handgun. "They got these when they got married," she said. "My grandparents gave them His and Hers guns. I don't know if they ever used them."

Clayton whistled soft and low. He hefted a big carbine off the rack. "What exactly did your dad hunt? Elephants?"

Kenzie shook her head. "Elk. Moose. The usual."

Clayton put the carbine back. "Wow. I'm impressed."

"He told me if I ever needed protection, I should use the little twelve-gauge," she said. "That way, I didn't have to be a sharpshooter to do some damage."

"I like the way he thinks. Let's get a couple of these out and loaded. Just in case. Does Todd own a gun?"

"I think so, but I only saw it when his lowlife friends were around, so I don't know if it was actually his or if they were just loaning it to him."

"Interesting," muttered Clayton. He was still transfixed by the gun collection. "Your dad collected all these weapons?"

"No, not all of them. At least half of these rifles belong to my brothers. My sister was into archery." She pointed at the modern crossbow in the corner.

"Holy moly. If I had know about all this before I met you, I don't think I would have had the courage to talk to you."

Kenzie grinned. "Don't worry. Daddy hardly ever shoots people."

"Hardly ever, huh? Glad to hear it."

Kenzie collected the twelve-gauge and a box of shells. Clayton took a deer rifle, the only firearm he had experience with. They moved their weapons to the kitchen table.

"I'm probably overreacting," he said, "but your house is twenty minutes from everything."

"You said you're calling Hutch. What can he do for us?"

Clayton stared at the contacts on his phone. "I'm hoping he and Thor will have some ideas. They didn't have much time to fill me in, what with all the kids around and Aunt Polly to deal with."

"She's a peach," said Kenzie darkly.

Clayton reassured her. "She has her good points. Nosiness and bossiness are not on that list." He frowned at the tiny screen. "I could have sworn I put Hutch's contact info in here. Maybe I should just call the police."

"No, please! The Mustang—"

He jumped a foot when the landline rang.

Kenzie made a face. She'd been startled too. She pulled the handset off the kitchen wall. "Hello?"

"It's Doreen Patterson. I just heard the news about your mother."

"That was fast," said Kenzie shakily.

"My sister works in the ER. What do you need? What can we do for you?"

"I'm not exactly sure. I'm in shock at the moment. Dad seems to think she'll be all right. He said something about them putting in stents in the morning. I'm not sure what we need, frankly. It's just me and my friend Clayton at the house. Someone's got to stay home and take care of the animals."

Clayton gestured for her to hand him the phone. She did so, and he spoke into it. "This is Clayton."

Mrs. Patterson chatted at him a while. Clayton nodded and replied with vague sounds, along with a few affirmatives and a few negatives. He motioned to Kenzie that he needed a pen and paper. When she complied, he jotted down several names and numbers. Then he handed the phone back to Kenzie. "She wants to talk to you a bit."

Kenzie sagged onto a kitchen chair. "Hi again."

"Sweetheart, don't you worry about a thing. Andy is in the other room talking to Thor Garrison. Thor called and said you might need some help with a situation you're in."

Kenzie stuttered, not knowing how much to tell her about Todd, the car, and the money. "I—I—I guess I could use some help." She laid a hand on one of the shotguns on the table.

"I was telling your friend Clayton how much your parents helped us out when Andy got kicked by that bull. Did your mother tell you about that? We were going to lose everything, and your folks took a second out on their farm because no one would loan to us. They saved us in our darkest hour. I gave Clayton a few names and numbers to call. It's hard for Andy to get around, so he's going to stay here and field phone calls. Meanwhile, I'm on my way over with warm bread, and I'm prepared to stay as long as you need me."

Kenzie wanted to speak, but no words would come, only tears of gratitude. She choked out the words, "Thank you so much."

"I'm on my way. Trust in the Lord, Kenzie dear. That's what we did when Andy was hurt, and what do you know? The Lord sent angels in the form of John and Marigold. Now it's our turn. You can hang up the phone now." She ended the call.

Kenzie gazed up at Clayton through her tears. "I wondered why Mom and Dad took out a mortgage on the farm. They were saving the Pattersons."

"I have a sneaking hunch they've helped out a lot of people over the years. Mrs. Patterson told me to call everyone on this list."

Kenzie wiped the tears off her cheeks and peered at the list. "Oh my. The Finemans? The McAvoys? The Feltons? George and Faith Washburn? The Darbys?"

Outside, the dogs started barking. Clayton picked up a shotgun and went to look out a window. A few moments later, someone knocked at the front door and he moved toward it. Kenzie followed him, saying, "Good grief, there's half the town on this piece of paper."

Clayton replied, "And it looks like they're all coming down your driveway."

Chapter Eighteen

BY NINE P.M., THE LIVING room and dining room were full of people. Kenzie could remember a time, back when she was still in elementary school, when her parents would have people over several times a year. As life wore on and became more complicated, those events dwindled. By the time Kenzie was a junior in high school, they had stopped altogether. She was overwhelmed now by the number of visitors in the house.

Fortunately, the women had each prepared something. As good as her word, Doreen Patterson brought warm homemade bread. Krystal Fineman and her new husband, Zachary King, brought three different dishes.

"This one is out of the freezer, Kenzie dear, and should go in the oven," said Krystal. "How is your mother doing?"

Kenzie took the proffered dish and stammered, "F-f-fine. I mean, stable. Surgery in the morning."

Doreen silently took the dish from Kenzie's hands and motioned with her head for Zach to follow with his armful.

Krystal gave Kenzie a careful hug and a peck on the cheek. "I'm sure she'll do well. Did your mother ever tell you we were locker mates in gym class? It feels like a lifetime ago." She paused, then added, "Oh my, it really was a lifetime ago, wasn't it?"

From somewhere deep inside, Kenzie pulled a memory out of storage and found herself using her mother's own words. "It's so lovely of you to come, Krystal. I hope you're feeling better these days. Mother mentioned that you had a weak spell a while back."

Krystal's gray eyes twinkled. "Did she, now?" The corners of her mouth turned up in a tiny smile, and her eyes filled with kindness. "Marigold and I were best friends in high school. I can't imagine a universe without her in it. When my first marriage was in trouble, she called me often, and it was she who convinced me to bring my family back to Colorado. I wish we had known sooner that they were having a hard time making ends meet. They never complained about anything." She covered Kenzie's hand with both of hers and squeezed gently.

Zach returned to Krystal's side, his weatherworn tan a sharp contrast to her pale complexion. "You tell your father he can have those cattle back whenever he wants. They're all fattened up now."

"But he sold them to you." Kenzie frowned.

Zach fiddled with his Stetson. "I know, but heck, we been using them for breeding, and I'm sure the stud fees and new calves would more than cover what we paid for them."

The McAvoys brought along a young man in a white coat and chef's hat, and Alice Kate directed him as he laid out their hot covered dishes. Reese took Kenzie's hand. She could have sworn he was taller before she went away to college.

"Sweet little Kenzie," he murmured, then wagged a finger. "I remember your senior prom. You looked like a queen surrounded by her subjects that night. And I don't think the prom queen ever got over having you steal the show."

Kenzie was taken aback. "I wasn't trying to steal anything."

"I know, I know. You never did see yourself as others saw you. I remember your mother when she was your age. Looking at you is like peeking through the window of a time machine."

Kenzie wasn't sure what to say. At last, she managed, "It was so kind of you to move our prom to your ballroom that year. It rained so hard that spring. Who knew there was a huge hole in the roof of the gym?"

Reese smiled, showing the gap in his front teeth. "Your dad was one of the first to volunteer over there, getting that roof fixed before graduation. He never failed to help out a neighbor. He was the one who urged me to talk to the town council about expanding the hotel, and then he started bringing in funding from folks around town. I never realized how many people he knew."

Kenzie smiled weakly. "They used to have big parties," she said lamely. She herself had never thought much about all the neighbors dropping by, each with their own problem. One by one, her dad would either lend a hand or give advice. Didn't everyone do that? How many other aspects of her parents had she taken for granted?

Taylor and Axel Garrison approached to offer their support. Taylor said, "Don't worry about work tomorrow. Sunny said she would cover for you."

Right behind her, Sunny piped up, "Brady told me how great your folks were to him when his uncle died and left him the garage. I guess his uncle and your dad's family were great friends. Your dad signed over his twenty percent of the garage to Brady so he could own the whole thing. He said he only bought in so the place wouldn't close down when Brady's uncle got too old to really do it all. That's why he wanted Brady here. Lucky for me." She tossed her hair back and gazed adoringly at her husband, who was chatting with Reese.

Thor Garrison, Austin Masters, and one of Doreen's daughters, Darlene, a pudgy, athletic woman in a deputy sheriff's uniform, filed by, each with a story about her parents and each offering to do whatever they could.

Kenzie felt as though she were walking through a kaleidoscope world of remembered kindnesses and debts owed. When Clayton brought her a plate of food, she just stood there, staring at it.

Clayton leaned close and said, "Use the fork. That's how most people get started."

Kenzie blinked up at him. "How could I be so oblivious to my parents' world?"

Clayton put an arm around her shoulders. "I don't think any of us really know our parents as people. Just Mom and Dad." He humphed thoughtfully. "I know there are things in my father's past...things about my mother, and my godmother, Lulamae...that he can't bear to talk about." He squeezed her gently. "Maybe I should back off and let him tell me in his own time."

Kenzie smiled. "I guess so." She pushed a green bean around the plate with her fork. "When that call came about them being at the ER? I thought it was my dad. He's the one who's been so sick and weak." She shook her head. "Mom just looked tired to me." She felt guilty that she hadn't been able to tell.

"Don't feel bad. They probably conspired to keep lots of truths from you. Parents do that. When things are really awful..." He flashed back to the day his father told them their mother was gone. Lulamae was standing in the doorway, biting her lip, and looking...tortured? Well, she and his mother had been close all their lives.

Kenzie nudged at him with her plate. "I can't really eat right now," she confessed. She glanced at the wall clock as Clayton set her plate on the the table. "Wasn't Dad going to call and give us an update on Mom's condition?"

No sooner had she voiced it than the phone rang. Clayton answered it and handed it to Kenzie. "It's your dad."

Kenzie took a deep breath and clutched the phone like a lifeline. "Dad? Is she still doing okay?"

John's voice sounded stronger than it had since she'd come home. "She's quite the fighter," he said. "She woke up a little bit ago and told me to go home and get some sleep."

"Are you going to do that?"

"Hell no. The nurses already put an extra bed in her room for me. I went to school with four or five of them." His voice dropped a bit. "Dated two of them before I met your mother." He chuckled.

Kenzie was confused. She'd never heard her father talk about such things. "Dad, should you be joking around at a time like this?"

Her father's voice grew more serious. "Kenzie, honey, your mother and I share a lot of history. We used to joke around all the time. It's the best way to face adversity. Pretend you're laughing. If Bad Luck thinks you're enjoying yourself, he'll give up and go bother someone else. Your mother used to say that all the time." He added wistfully, "Then she slowed down. Got tired. I should have made her get a check-up."

Kenzie forced some cheer into her voice. "Don't go shouldering blame, Dad. I've been doing that all evening. I've got that one covered."

"You're a good girl, Kenzie. See you in the morning?"

"Of course."

"Surgery's scheduled for 8 a.m. Plenty of time to see to the animals."

Kenzie smiled. Now *that* was the father she remembered. "I'll be there, Dad. Don't worry."

She hung up the phone and felt as if her last ounce of strength had left her. "Clayton? Would you mind playing host? I need to lie down."

"Go on up to bed," he said gently. "After everyone leaves, I'll sleep on the couch."

"My brothers' rooms are upstairs at the front of the house. I'm sure they wouldn't mind if you slept there."

"Thanks." He kissed her softly. "Now go on. I've got some things to take care of."

Kenzie wanted to ask him what sort of things, but her brain wouldn't focus. She nodded and trudged up the stairs. The room fell quiet for a few moments as everyone watched her slow ascent. She closed her bedroom door and moved zombie-like to the bed. She sat on the edge of it and picked up the little porcelain figures Clayton had given her. She pressed them to her lips and kissed them good night. Then she placed them under her pillow and lay down fully clothed. She didn't have the strength to go back down and fetch her cell phone. She'd have to charge it in the morning. Her last waking thought was that her mother would have scolded her to put on her jammies.

♡

Clayton spotted Kenzie's phone and picked it up. He ran a hand over his forehead and wondered how much of Kenzie's problem he should share with these friends and neighbors.

Doreen Patterson made the decision for him. She brought him a cup of coffee, and settled at the dining room table. "Clayton, does this trouble of Kenzie's have anything to do with that smashed Mustang over at the quarry?"

Clayton stammered with surprise. "You…you know about that?" He glanced around the room, realizing that everyone was listening.

Doreen shrugged. "I know about the car because Darlene here came over for dinner and mentioned she'd seen a new abandoned vehicle when she checked on our property. Andy's father left him the quarry, which was closed for business before he inherited it. We tried selling it when Andy got hurt, but no one wanted it. The Shanes were so sweet. They told Andy that they would accept the old quarry as collateral on that loan."

Clayton's eyebrows met. He addressed Darlene. "As a deputy sheriff, did you have to report to someone about that car?"

Darlene shrugged. Years of working among male officers had put some swagger in her tone. "No need. It's on private property. I checked to see if anyone had reported it missing, and I told my folks it was there. But Dad wasn't worried about it. He's too busy getting ready for a big leatherwork shipment to a stable in New York City. So we left it alone."

Clayton fiddled with Kenzie's phone. After a few seconds, he realized that everyone in the room was gathering around and waiting for him to speak, so he did. "Look, everyone, I'm really fond of Kenzie."

Axel and Taylor exchanged a smile. "Yeah," said Axel, "we could kind of tell."

"She came home to help her folks, but she left a bad situation in Denver. It turns out…I hope she'll forgive me for sharing this, but…Todd, the man she fell in love with in college, turned out to be a really bad dude. Or at least, that seems to be his career aspiration. He put Kenzie in debt and lied to her about everything. When her mother asked her to come home and help out, she took his Mustang in order to get home, and then…well, she told me she was so hurt, she wasn't thinking straight. She wanted revenge on Todd, so she pushed the Mustang over the cliff.

"Ever since she arrived, Todd has been threatening her, and now…." He lifted Kenzie's phone in the air. "Now he's threatening to come after her. He figured out where she is."

Darlene prepared a forkful of cake for consumption, but before she popped it into her mouth, she said, "Interesting. He never reported the car missing."

"And we think we know why," said Clayton. "I went down there with Kenzie because we thought it was strange that he hadn't sicced the law on her for taking the car. And we found over a hundred thousand dollars in the trunk."

A murmur raced around the room.

"Where is it now?" asked Darlene.

"We took it out of the trunk and hid it in a slag heap. Thor and Ryan Hutch are investigating what Todd did to collect that much money. Kenzie was terrified she'd be hauled into some criminal mess."

Darlene swallowed cake. "Maybe my folks don't want that car in the quarry. And since Kenzie's folks have an interest in the place now, maybe they don't want it there either." She prepared another bite of cake.

Clayton frowned. "I don't get it."

Doreen leaned back in her chair and seemed to pick up on her daughter's train of thought. "Brady? Don't you have a front loader for sale over at the garage?"

Brady nodded. "Yep. Sure do."

Clayton frowned, still trying to figure out where this conversation was going.

"Well, Andy and I have a big old backhoe that just sits out at the quarry. I wonder if it still runs?"

A smile crept across Brady's face. "Maybe we should find out."

Doreen nodded. "Good. We'll need both of them. This here ex-boyfriend can't have Kenzie arrested for stealing a car that ain't there, now, can he?"

The light began to dawn for Clayton. "Are you thinking of moving it?"

Brady made eye contact with several of the men in the room. "Oh, we have a few ideas. Mainly, first thing in the morning, I say we take that front loader down to the quarry and put it through its paces."

The group liked that idea a lot.

Axel raised a hand. "Is this ex-boyfriend a nuisance? Or is he real trouble?"

Clayton lifted Kenzie's phone in the air. "I'll let you decide." He powered it up and shared the last ten messages from Todd.

Taylor clasped Axel's arm. "She must be terrified."

Darlene set her fork down long enough to peer at the phone. "Humph. Did you leave all that money hidden down there?"

"Yes," said Clayton. Then he remembered. "No! Kenzie brought a bundle home to her mother. She thought one reason she was so exhausted was from worrying about money. She left it in the fridge."

Axel frowned. "Why the heck—"

But all the women nodded. "Perfect place to make sure her mother found it."

Darlene stood up and straightened her weapons belt. "Is it still there?"

Clayton went to look. Darlene was right behind him, and the others straggled after. He spotted the cash in a fat envelope behind a dish of leftover green beans and pulled it out.

A murmur went through the group.

Darlene said, "Do you mind if I take this? Run a few checks on the serial numbers?"

"No, not at all. I'll explain to Kenzie in the morning."

"Meanwhile," said Darlene, "if this guy shows up here at the house, what's the plan?" She let her gaze settle on the guns on the kitchen table. "You taking him hunting?"

Clayton almost laughed. "No. I just—the farm is kind of isolated and…." He let it trail off as a chuckle rippled through the group.

Perky Erin Masters chirped, "It felt that way to me, too, when I first moved here. But don't be fooled. Eagle's Toe is smack dab in the middle of the twenty-first century." She pulled out her cell, and several others followed suit.

Doreen nodded and offered, "Make one of them there message lists so you can reach everyone at the same time."

After a few minutes of everyone talking at once to get the list set up, Clayton looked around the group. "Everyone covered?"

Darlene said, "Test it."

Clayton typed the message. "Everyone covered?"

A room full of phones beeped and chimed, followed by a chorus of "Got it."

"Good." Clayton juggled his phone and Kenzie's, stuffing them in a pocket.

Darlene said, "Leave her phone on. This yahoo thinks he's scaring her, so he'll probably keep sending threats until he actually gets here."

"And then what?" asked Clayton.

"First," said Darlene, "put these guns away. You don't look like much of a hunter to me. And second, come into the dining room. You need a plan. If anyone asks you about it later, say my mother came up with it. Ordinarily, I'd be telling you to call 911 if he shows his face around here."

Clayton paused. "Should we?"

"No. I'll get the message on my phone, like everyone else. That will alert us all."

"Will you get in trouble for this?"

Darlene shrugged. "My uncle is the sheriff. We flipped a coin about which one would come out here. So I'm not worried. If we need backup, I'll call from my patrol car. Now listen up, everybody. If we get that message…just send HELP," she added for Clayton's benefit, "…here's what we're going to do."

Chapter Nineteen

KENZIE AWOKE IN THE morning to the smell of freshly brewed coffee. A few moments later, there was a tap at her door.

"Come in!"

Clayton entered with a tray. He said, "I thought you might enjoy coffee in bed for a change. I assume this is not your usual start to the morning, but I'm hoping to make an extremely good impression."

Kenzie laughed briefly, then remembered everything that had gone on the day before and fell silent.

Clayton said, "If you like, I can be feeding the animals myself. And then we'll go to the hospital."

Kenzie shook her head. "Communing with animals is what's been keeping me sane, along with your company, of course."

Clayton tilted his head to one side. "You slept in your clothes."

Kenzie looked down at herself as she maneuvered into a sitting position so Clayton could deposit the tray over her lap. "Too tired to change last night. Two cups? I hope that means you're having coffee with me."

"I wouldn't miss it for the world," said Clayton softly.

"How late did everyone stay?"

"Until eleven or so." He poured coffee carefully into both cups. "Sugar? Milk?"

"Just sugar." Kenzie felt her tension easing as Clayton fussed over her. "I just don't get it," she said.

"Don't get what?" asked Clayton, smiling sweetly.

"I just can't believe that you aren't already taken."

Clayton puffed up a bit. "I assume you mean in the sense of marriage, not in the sense of a Liam Neeson movie."

Kenzie laughed again, then caught herself. "Oh my gosh, how are you able to make me laugh on the morning of my mother's surgery?" She reached out and touched his hand. "When I came to bed last night, I was afraid I would never laugh again."

Clayton pretended to jot a note down on the knee of his jeans. "Note to self: Able to make her laugh in the face of adversity, 20 points."

Kenzie smiled and sipped her coffee. For a few seconds, the two of them sat there holding hands and saying nothing. At last, Clayton cleared his throat and said, "I better get out of here so you can get dressed. I mean, changed."

"I guess so," said Kenzie, "although I should probably feed the animals in this outfit and clean up afterwards."

It proved to be the right decision because the pigs wanted petting and the goats wanted to play and the chickens needed feeding and no one had cleaned the coop for a while. Kenzie allowed herself to get lost in the mundane chores of tending to the animals. They were such sweet souls and so peaceful. They didn't know that her mother would be on the operating table this morning. And maybe that was for the best.

They arrived at the hospital at seven forty-five. They went straight to her mother's room, but she was already gone. Her father was waiting for them there.

"The doctor said we should go to the waiting room outside the surgery. They said they would move her to recovery after she comes out and give her a new room later." John sounded tired and confused. Kenzie gave him a big hug. "It must've been a very long night," she said.

John nodded. "But the doctor said everything is going according to plan. They came and got her at six to prep for surgery." He seemed unable to move.

Kenzie was relieved when Clayton took charge. "Let's head to the waiting room."

"Good idea," said Kenzie, secretly concerned about her father's mental state. "We'll stay with you, Dad. Every minute. And don't worry, the animals are fine."

For the next three hours, Kenzie's universe was limited to plastic chairs, a linoleum floor, and holding hands with the only two men in her life that she trusted completely. Clayton was a strong arm to lean on when she needed one most. He never left her side, except for a brief trip to the men's room. When he returned, he said softly, "You should have told me I made that coffee too strong."

They all tried to laugh.

When the doctor came through the door, they stood up, waiting to learn if their lives would ever be the same.

"Everything went great," he began.

Kenzie, John, and Clayton shared a group hug.

As the doctor kept talking, Kenzie nodded and tried to keep up, but she was so flooded with relief, she wasn't sure she understood much. "When can we see her?"

"She's in Recovery right now. John, I'm going to have the nurses show you to her new room on the cardiac floor. You can wait for her there. If you like, we'll arrange for you to stay over again tonight."

"Good. Okay. Thanks, Paul. So glad you made it through med school. You saved her life."

The doctor smiled warmly. "Bet you never thought that summer job would come to this," he said gently, gesturing at his surgical scrubs. "Consider it a thank you gift. If you want to talk to me, the floor nurses will page me." He shook John's hand, then left.

Kenzie moved her gaze back and forth between her dad and the doctor's back. "You know him?"

"Remember that college student who spent summers working the farm when you were in junior high? That was Paul. When he came up short on med school tuition, your mother and I offered a helping hand."

"Wow." Kenzie shook her head. "When Mom is well enough to come home, you two need to fill me in on your secret lives."

"No secret," said John. "Just neighbor helping neighbor." He glanced around at the empty chairs, and his tone wobbled. "Guess I thought one or two of them might come over and wait with us." He looked away.

Clayton laid a firm hand on his shoulder. "Don't worry, John. They were all at your house last night, and I think they've got a few surprises for you. They figured Kenzie and I would be here, so they could help out their neighbor elsewhere."

John looked puzzled. "Kenzie? You know I hate surprises."

Kenzie laughed, and her relief was so total that she found it hard to stop. She never saw the tears coming, but when they did, Clayton wrapped her in his arms and murmured, "It's all right, sweetheart. Everything will be all right."

♡

Clayton convinced John to let him buy lunch, but the older man would only agree if they ate it in the room where he was waiting for his wife. Neither John nor Kenzie finished their hamburgers. When Paul dropped by personally to escort John to Recovery after Marigold woke up, Clayton murmured to Kenzie, "We need to take care of some things while your dad is occupied."

He was pleased when Kenzie didn't hesitate. She kissed her dad and told him they would check back later. "Call us when Mom is in her room, if you think she can stand to see us for a bit."

Downstairs in the Mercedes, Clayton started the engine before showing Kenzie her phone. "Todd is not a nice man."

Kenzie began to read the most recent message, but rolled her eyes and dropped the phone in the cup holder. "That part of my life feels a hundred years away."

"Don't let your guard down yet. Darlene texted me earlier that a man on a motorcycle was spotted on the road between Pueblo and Eagle's Toe. He fit Todd's description."

Kenzie closed her eyes. "When will it ever end?"

"Soon," said Clayton calmly. He glanced sideways at her and flashed an impish smile. "After you went to bed last night, some of us came up with a plan."

Kenzie straightened up and opened her eyes. "What plan?"

"You'll see." Clayton was grinning now, but forced himself to stop talking before he could give anything away. "Just promise me that you will trust me and follow my lead when Todd shows up."

Kenzie nodded and slipped her hand under his arm. "I will." She pulled back abruptly. "How did she get Todd's description?"

Clayton felt his color rising. "I, um, well, I had to show them the messages on your phone so they'd know what we're dealing with. And Darlene asked if you had any photos of him." He cringed, waiting for her to explode.

Instead, she leaned against his arm again. "Okay. That makes sense."

Clayton was amazed. Not only was she beautiful, she was the most reasonable woman he'd ever met. He grinned like a man in love.

His smile disappeared when they turned onto the long gravel driveway to the farmhouse. The paint crew he was hoping to surprise Kenzie with was loitering about their truck. Out in front of the house, Todd straddled his motorcycle, leaning back, arms crossed. Waiting. On the porch, the dogs were barking non-stop. They fell silent when they recognized the occupants of the Mercedes.

"Uh-oh," said Kenzie.

"Be calm," said Clayton softly. He drove slowly toward the motorcycle, glancing into his lap as he did so to type something on his phone. "Hit send for me, will you?"

146

Kenzie took the phone and hit send. Then she shot him a questioning glance. "HELP? That's your message? Who did you send it to?"

Clayton smiled grimly. "You'll see. Play along, okay?"

"Yeah. Sure." Kenzie looked half scared, half befuddled.

Clayton stopped the car and got out, motioning for Kenzie to stay put. He addressed Todd, loudly and clearly. "You must be the ex."

Todd sneered at him. "I'm done with her," he spat. "I just want my car back." He spewed a string of insults and let them hang in the air.

"That's no way for a gentleman to talk," said Clayton. He nodded at the painting crew, who slowly went back to work. Then he pinned Todd with a hard stare. "If I take you to the spot where Kenzie left your car, will you disappear and never come back?"

Todd snorted in disgust. "Maybe." He was trying to look as tough as he could, but his long, lean, bad-boy style just made him look scrawny next to Clayton's wholesome muscle.

Clayton said coldly, "The correct answer is yes."

"Ha! Take me to my car." He fiddled with something stuffed into the waistband of his jeans.

"Follow me," said Clayton. He got back into the Mercedes and turned it carefully around.

"What are you doing?!" Kenzie sounded panicked.

"Have faith." Clayton checked his mirror to make sure Todd was following.

Kenzie glanced back, then noted, "You hired a crew to paint the house!"

"Surprise," said Clayton, not breaking his concentration. Then he added sweetly, "Consider it a gift." Out on the highway, he went ten miles below the speed limit, making sure Todd didn't get lost.

A large black SUV pulled around both Todd and the Mercedes and sped on down the road.

Kenzie cocked her head. "Hey, isn't that Thor's vehicle?"

"Was it? Well, you know. Small town." He took a peek at Kenzie to see how she was doing. He could tell from her expression that she was working on it. She hadn't figured it out yet, but she peered at him with serious curiosity. All her fear was gone.

"Where are we going?"

Clayton said, "We're taking Todd to the spot where you left his car."

"Right." She drew the word out into an accusation. "Okay." She glanced backward. "He's still following."

"Could you tell if he was carrying a gun?"

Kenzie took a deep breath. "When he played with one, he always tucked it into his pants. I told him once he might shoot off something he'd regret. So yes, I think he has one."

"Good. We agree. I saw him tucking something into his jeans. If you hear a gunshot, drop flat on the ground. Understood?"

Kenzie nodded and swallowed hard.

Clayton turned off on Old Quarry Road, moving even slower on the gravel. The breeze seemed to pick up dust clouds around the rim of the pit.

"Uh-oh," he said, checking his mirror.

Todd was zooming up alongside him. "Pull over!"

Clayton hesitated, then stopped. He lowered his window a couple of inches. "What's the problem?"

"Are you yanking my chain? Kenzie! If you're trying to pull something…."

Kenzie shouted back, "Do you want your stupid car or not?"

Todd sat for a minute, trying to gauge her response. At last, he grumbled. "All right, but no funny stuff. I got a gun."

"Nothing funny here," mumbled Clayton as he began moving again.

Todd followed just far enough behind to avoid most of their dust.

When Clayton reached the spot where Kenzie had shoved the car over the rim, he made a left-hand turn and followed the ruts around the edge.

"What's going on?" asked Kenzie.

"Like I said. We're taking him to the spot where you left his car."

"Oh my gosh. You know it's going to hit the fan, right? When he sees the wreck?"

Clayton said softly, "Oh ye of little faith."

Thanks to some directions from Doreen the night before, Clayton knew to follow Old Quarry Road to the left instead of the right. This side of the road was well kept and meandered downwards toward the mouth of the pit, opposite the spot where Kenzie had pushed the car over. At the gate, there was a faded sign proclaiming, "Patterson Quarry. No trespassing." The gate stood open and Clayton did not slow down.

"Who opened the gate?" asked Kenzie, looking all around.

"Don't give anything away," said Clayton. "Look straight ahead." He drove to the spot near the back of the quarry where they had buried the money. Off to the left was a large backhoe. Some distance away to the right was a front loader with its big shovel perched in the air. The slag piles stood silent watch as Clayton stopped the car. The earth at the bottom of the cliff was flat and empty, criss-crossed with giant tire tracks.

Kenzie whispered, "Where's the car?"

"Stay right next to me," said Clayton.

Kenzie nodded. She got out of the Mercedes and moved quickly to his side. Together, they faced their adversary.

Todd made a show of revving his engine before shutting the bike down and dismounting. He hooked his thumbs in his belt loops, inches from the handle of the firearm that protruded from his jeans. "Well?! Where the hell is it?"

"Kenzie left it right there." Clayton pointed to the newly flattened earth.

"Where is it *now!?*" Todd was red in the face. "Kenzie! Where's my car?"

Kenzie shrugged. "I left it right here. Someone must have stolen it."

Todd screamed obscenities at her and pulled out his pistol.

At that moment, a sheriff's car swerved around a slag pile, its siren blaring. Todd whirled around, clearly unsure what to do with his gun.

The siren stopped, and Deputy Sheriff Darlene Patterson got out of the vehicle. "Todd Wilson?" She didn't even need a megaphone in the pit. Sound carried and bounced off the cliff walls. "Are you Todd Wilson?" She lifted her hands over the driver's side door, revealing her service Special. She aimed it at Todd.

All the color in Todd's face drained away. He tossed his gun on the ground and held his hands so high, his jeans threatened to fall to his knees. "What do you want?" he yelled.

From behind slag heap after slag heap, people began appearing. The Garrison men, the Masters brothers, Zachary King and some ranch hands, and many more. They formed a slowly closing circle around Todd. And every one of them was carrying a weapon. Some had rifles. Some had pitchforks. Reese McAvoy carried a large cleaver.

Todd seemed to shrink where he stood.

Clayton demanded, "Are you missing a car or not?"

Todd looked confused. "Yes, dammit. That dang girl stole it!"

Deputy Darlene looked around. "Stole what?"

Todd was fit to be tied. "This is a trick! I want a lawyer!"

Ryan Hutch approached, carrying a tennis racquet. "Sorry. I'm already representing Kenzie."

"Where's my car?!"

"No car has been reported stolen," said Darlene. "No report, no car theft."

Todd stamped his feet and swore a blue streak.

Clayton held up a finger. "Oh, I bet he had something inside this missing car."

Todd's color returned as two spots of red on his cheeks. He looked like he might explode any moment. "What are you talking about?"

Darlene said, "The bills Kenzie found. The ones with your fingerprints all over them. Did you ever tell Kenzie you were arrested for robbing a gas station? Your prints are on file."

"I don't know anything...." Todd could barely force himself to finish. "...about no money." He practically choked on the word.

"No kidding?" Darlene was having fun now. "The serial numbers match those from a bank robbery. Three million dollars, and all you got was a hundred thousand? You must not have been very important to your fellow thieves."

Now Todd was working his fists, and he glanced hungrily at the pistol on the ground.

Everyone carrying a rifle raised and pointed it.

"Don't even try it," said Darlene. "Todd Wilson, you are under arrest for bank robbery, stalking, and threatening harm to Kenzie Shane. We don't hold with that here."

Todd looked sick. "This is...this is entrapment! You can't arrest me! You got no warrant."

Clayton looked smug. "Citizens' arrest. All these citizens are arresting you for giving the wrong woman a very hard time. And, of course, for bank robbery."

Darlene reached into her car for her radio and called for backup.

Kenzie asked, "Do you really need backup?"

Darlene gave a little shrug. "My uncle didn't want to miss out on the action."

"I'll deny everything!" shouted Todd.

Clayton said, "Dude, she has your fingerprints all over the money. Money we found in the trunk of your car. You're toast."

"Oh yeah?! Then shoot me! Come on you cowards, shoot me!"

Nobody moved. A moment later, the sound of another siren could be heard, approaching at a fast clip.

"Hands behind your back," said Darlene. She fastened the plastic cuffs to his wrists.

Todd sounded like a whiney schoolboy. "Where's my car?"

Clayton said, "You'll find out at the trial."

Kenzie shook her head. "What did I ever see in you?" She wrapped an arm around Clayton's waist and gazed up at him. "I guess once you meet a real man, there's no going back."

Todd sputtered, "I hate you, Kenzie Shane, you—"

Darlene cut him off. "You'll have plenty of time to think about that," she said. "Lots and lots of time." She grabbed his arm and put him in her patrol car.

Kenzie made a sound.

Clayton said, "Did you just giggle?"

She squeezed him. "I feel lighter than air!" She looked at the faces of the crowd, each of them sending affectionate looks back. "You all were fantastic! How did you do this? And how did you resist shooting him?"

Thor Garrison winked at her. "Our guns aren't loaded."

Kenzie gaped.

They all laughed.

"So where is the car?" she asked.

The group exchanged glances, but no one spoke. Ryan Hutch said calmly, "What car? Todd's car? I heard that someone stole it."

"Will he press charges?" She sucked in air as she spoke.

"He'll be way too busy defending himself and turning state's evidence against his accomplices. And we'll make sure he has an incentive not to press charges."

Kenzie leaned into Clayton. "You did this, didn't you?"

Clayton wrapped his arms around her. "I love you, Kenzie Shane. I couldn't help myself."

Kenzie's expression melted into adoration. "I love you, too, Clayton. Say you'll never leave me."

"I'll never leave you," he murmured. "Will you marry me?"

Kenzie wrapped her arms around his neck and kissed him on the mouth. The crowd cheered. Startled, Kenzie broke off the kiss, and replied, "Yes, Clayton. Yes." She pressed her mouth close to his ear and whispered, "Where's the evidence?"

Clayton whispered back. "The money's in the front loader, and you're standing on the car."

Kenzie shrieked for joy and kissed him again. "What a great wedding gift!"

Epilogue

Eight months later

CLAYTON TOOK A DEEP BREATH. "What is that heavenly scent?"

Marigold waved a hand. "My mother's catalpa trees. This is why Kenzie chose to have a June wedding. The catalpas are in bloom." She inhaled deeply. "Reminds me of my own wedding."

"Oh, right. Kenzie told me they'd be a sight to see." He fidgeted with his tie. "Isn't it time yet?"

Marigold smiled. "Don't be in such a rush. She won't change her mind."

For a millisecond, a flash of terror shot through Clayton. Then he realized he was being teased. "Good." He nodded, struck nearly dumb by the import of the day.

Marigold squeezed his hand. "John and I are so happy to have you join the family."

"Thanks," said Clayton. "At least the bride's side will fill the chairs."

Marigold raised her brows. "Don't be so quick to count out your own flesh and blood. All your cousins are already here." She raised the cane in her left hand like a salute in response to Belle and Uly Garrison's wave.

Clayton checked his phone. "We're already running twenty minutes late. I hope the pastor doesn't give up and leave. You said Kenzie was ready ten minutes early. What's the hold up?"

Plano Masters' deep voice came from behind him. "Me! I'm the hold up, you rambunctious pup."

Clayton whirled. "Dad! How did you get here?"

152

"Almost didn't. Got lost on the way out here. Lucky for you, Austin decided this was an event I shouldn't miss." He tossed his head back. "He convinced me that you wanted me here. Should I go back to the hotel?"

Clayton grabbed his father in a bear hug. The feelings that welled up caught him by surprise. After a few seconds of vice-like grip, he let his father breathe. "Remind me to thank Austin," he mumbled.

Plano laughed. "I can't believe we actually surprised you. I've already met my in-laws," he said graciously, lifting Marigold's hand to his lips for a kiss.

John Shane, resplendent in a tailored tuxedo, grumbled playfully, "Look out, Goldie. He's flirting with you."

Plano and John shook hands.

"I'm really glad to see you, Dad," said Clayton.

Plano harrumphed. "Austin said you needed family at your wedding." He spread his arms. "You must have the entire population of Eagle's Toe here today. Where's an old man supposed to sit down?"

John matched Plano grumble for grumble. "For a billionaire, you don't seem too observant. There's a whole row of chairs waiting for you, right up front."

Lulamae Franklin's southern drawl caught Clayton off guard. "If you behave yourself, Plano, you can sit by me."

"Lulamae!" Clayton lifted her off the ground and spun her in the air.

She dropped her cane. "Easy, *cheri.* Easy."

John retrieved it for her.

"How…? When…?"

"Now, now," she said sweetly, "y'all can't be getting married without Lulamae. T'wouldn't be binding." She winked at him.

"Where's Tex?"

"He's working a deal in South Africa. We'll send him pictures of us all getting plowed at the reception."

Marigold laughed. "Oh my goodness. Lulamae, I think I like you."

Lulamae held up her cane. "The Sisterhood of the Lame Dames, that's us." She took a moment to stroke Clayton's cheek. "Our little Clay is getting married." She leaned close. "Your mama would be so proud." Before he could say anything, she turned to Marigold, "Now, where do y'all want us to sit, *cherie?*"

Clayton's heart was so full, he wasn't sure it would survive the wedding. He leaned toward Marigold. "Let's hope I don't need a couple stents of my own before the day is over." He glanced back at the house. "I'll be right back." He took off.

Behind him, Marigold cautioned him, "You're not supposed to see her in her dress yet."

Clayton called back, "I'll close my eyes!"

Inside the kitchen, he snagged a wedding cookie, then stepped into the living room. No Kenzie. He stood at the foot of the stairs. "Kenz? You ready?"

A moment later she peeked over the bannister from the landing. "Did your surprises get here?"

"Did everyone know but me?"

"Yes, silly. That's the definition of a surprise."

Clayton stood transfixed. "You look fantastic."

Kenzie was leaning her head around the corner, trying to keep her dress out of sight. "Well, at least my hair passes."

Clayton laughed. Then he ran up the stairs.

"What are you doing?" Kenzie feigned horror. "It's against the law to see me in my dress before the wedding."

But he was already there, wrapping her up in his arms. "Mmmm, you smell better than the catalpa blossoms."

Kenzie blushed. "That's not easy to do."

Clayton kissed her tenderly. "My father actually came to my wedding."

"Of course he did."

"And he brought Lulamae."

"You said she was like a second mother to you. I hope you're glad to see her."

"Just surprised, that's all. After all the fighting with my dad…."

"I know. Parents are like that. If mine could forgive me for all that stupidity in Denver, then I guess they can forgive anything."

Clayton could not pull his eyes away from her lips. "I hope we're that good when we're parents."

Kenzie's blush deepened. "Do you mind if we get married first?"

Clayton chuckled. "If you insist." He swept a stray lock of hair off her cheek.

Kenzie kissed his palm. "Austin said your father brought a third surprise. A wedding gift. He said it's already in your bank account."

Clayton nuzzled her cheek. "You are the only gift I'll ever need."

"I'm non-returnable."

"The best kind."

Kenzie pressed her fingers against his lips. "Go on downstairs," she said. "I can't wait to be Mrs. Mackenzie Masters."

Ashley Garrison's voice floated up from the kitchen as a piano began playing. "Clayton? Get down here! I'm bribing the ring bearer with jelly beans and I'm running out!"

Clayton forced himself to leave Kenzie on the stairs. He followed Ashley outside. The next thirty minutes were a total blur, like a dream, and when he woke, he was kissing his true love, Mrs. Mackenzie Shane Masters, amidst the cheers of family and friends.

Other Books by Regina Duke

The Wedding Wager (Colorado Billionaires, 1)
The Wedding Hope (Colorado Billionaires, 2)
The Wedding Venture (Colorado Billionaires, 3)
The Wedding Belle (Colorado Billionaires, 4)
The Wedding Guest (Colorado Billionaires, 5)
The Wedding Toast (Colorado Billionaires, 6)
The Wedding Gift (Colorado Billionaires, 7)
Colorado Billionaires Boxed Set (Contains novels 1, 2, and 3)
Colorado Billionaires Boxed Set 2 (Contains novels 4, 5, and 6)
Colorado Billionaires 8 Novellas (Contains: *Sunny's Christmas, Krystal's Christmas, Christmas Angel, Love Again, Twice the Joy, Jingle Bell Magic, Jingle Bell Wedding, Jingle Bell Romance*)
Colorado Billionaires Christmas 2014 (*Sunny's Christmas, Krystal's Christmas, Christmas Angel*)
Colorado Billionaires Christmas 2015 (*Jingle Bell Magic, Jingle Bell Wedding, Jingle Bell Romance*)
Love on the Lazy B: Love Again, Twice the Joy (Two Colorado Billionaires Stories)
Self-Help for Writers: Being Your Own Cheerleader
My Vampire Wedding
Trickster and Other Stories
Loving the Sensitive Dog

And from *Lovers Lane Romance*

North Rim Delight (Silver State Romance, 1)
The Woof in the Wedding Plans (Silver State Romance, 2)
Calin's Cowboy (Silver State Romance, 3)
Silver State Romance Boxed Set (Contains novels 1, 2, and 3)

If you enjoy Regina Duke's books, you will love Sandra Edwards' romances.

About Regina Duke

USA TODAY Bestselling Author Regina Duke writes sweet romance, cozy mystery, and paranormal. She lives in the High Desert with her three dogs, and when she's not writing she's playing the piano and enjoying her friends. For more info on Regina's books, visit her websites: ReginaDuke.com (fiction) and LindaLouWrites.com (non-fiction).

Visit the author at her author page http://www.amazon.com/Regina-Duke/e/B005KB08YM or email her at me@reginaduke.com.